Journey to the Imaginal Realm

*A Reader's Guide
to J. R. R. Tolkien's*
The Lord of the Rings

*A Nuralogical book,
produced in collaboration with Nura Learning
www.nuralearning.com*

Journey to the Imaginal Realm:

A Reader's Guide to J. R. R. Tolkien's The Lord of the Rings

Becca Tarnas

**REVELORE
MMXIX**

Journey to the Imaginal Realm:
A Reader's Guide to J. R. R. Tolkien's The Lord of the Rings

© Becca Tarnas 2019

All rights reserved. No part of this publication may be reproduced or utilized in any form or by any means, electronic or mechanical, including photocopying, recording, or by any information storage and retrieval system, without permission in writing from the Publishers.

Book and cover design by Jenn Zahrt.
Cover image and interior art by Arik Roper.

ISBN 978-1-947544-21-5

Printed globally on demand through IngramSpark

First printed by REVELORE PRESS in 2019

REVELORE PRESS
220 2ND AVE S #91
Seattle, WA 98104
USA

www.revelore.press

To my parents,
who raised me to trust the imagination.

Acknowledgments

When I wrote this book I did not even realize I had written a book. The text was born out of lectures crafted for my course "Journey to the Imaginal Realm: Reading J. R. R. Tolkien's *The Lord of the Rings*," hosted by Nura Learning. Thus, my first thanks must go to Jeremy Johnson, the founder of Nura Learning, for suggesting that these lectures merited becoming a published work. My deepest gratitude goes to Jenn Zahrt and Jeremy Johnson of Revelore Press, for their extraordinary editing skills, creative input, and clarity of vision.

Teaching the "Journey to the Imaginal Realm" course in the autumn of 2018 brought me into a community of lovers of Tolkien's work and deeply committed travelers of Middle-earth, which was an immensely gratifying experience. The students in the course provided intelligent and insightful dialogue which has gone on to shape the revisions of this text. Without their dedication and passion, this book certainly would not have come into existence. My special thanks also go to the close friends and family members who attended the course as well: Ashton Arnoldy, Laura Pustarfi, my mother and father, and my husband, Matthew Segall. It was always such a joy to see your faces in class and to hear your thoughts on Tolkien's legendarium.

I owe a debt of gratitude to my brother, Christopher Flash Tarnas, for giving me my first copy of *The Lord of the Rings*, and to my parents, Heather Malcolm and Richard Tarnas, for nourishing my imagination as a child and enthusiastically supporting me as I continued to study this field in graduate school and beyond. Furthermore, I am deeply thankful for all of my graduate professors at the California Institute of Integral Studies, particularly Jacob Sherman, who introduced me to the philosophy of imagination and demonstrated that it was possible to study Tolkien's work at a graduate level.

A book is never an individual effort, and my profound thanks go to all those dear to my heart who have provided support, care, and sheer encouragement throughout this process: Samuel Sohmer, Olga Sohmer, Lilly Falconer, Laura Michetti, and of course, Matt Segall.

Finally, to John Ronald Reuel Tolkien, for discovering the doorway to Middle-earth, and guiding us all on this journey into the world of the imagination.

Contents

Acknowledgments ~ vii
Preface ~ xi
A Biographical Introduction ~ xix

CHAPTER 1: ~ 1
The Fellowship of the Ring – Book I
From Hobbiton to Rivendell

INTERLUDE: ~ 21
Sub-Creation: Tolkien's
Philosophy of Imagination

CHAPTER 2: ~ 31
The Fellowship of the Ring – Book II
From the Misty Mountains to the Great River

INTERLUDE: ~ 65
The Book of Ishness and the Great War

CHAPTER 3: ~ 79
The Two Towers – Book III
From Rohan and Fangorn to Isengard

INTERLUDE: ~ 105
The Languages of Middle-Earth

CHAPTER 4: ~ 119
The Two Towers – Book IV
From the Emyn Muil to Cirith Ungol

INTERLUDE: ~ 143
The Myth of Creation and the Source of Evil

CHAPTER 5: ~ 151
The Return of the King – Book V
In the Land of Gondor

CHAPTER 6: ~ 179
The Return of the King – Book VI
From Mordor to the Grey Havens

Epilogue ~ 221
Bibliography ~ 225
About Nura Learning ~ 229

Preface

THE WORLD OF MIDDLE-EARTH is a place I have been wandering in my imagination for over two decades. I intend never to leave for long its hidden pathways, the secret roads that run under starlight, passing through forest and field, over mountains and across great rivers. Indeed, I have always wanted to share those journeys with others, passing back and forth across the threshold of the imagination in the company of fellows. Thus, when the opportunity arose to guide a class of students upon a journey through J. R. R. Tolkien's *The Lord of the Rings*, I knew I had many years of reflections, insights, research, and discoveries to share, as well as a desire for ongoing inquiry and communal contemplation. This reader's guide was born of those class lectures, and is designed both for newcomers to Tolkien's narrative and for veteran travelers through Middle-earth's many realms. This book explores the grand themes and quiet nuances of Tolkien's epic story, connecting *The Lord of the Rings* to the larger mythology of Middle-earth, and situating Tolkien's process of writing within his own powerful experiences of the imaginal realm.

This reader's guide is meant to be read in conjunction with *The Lord of the Rings*, as a companion book to Tolkien's text. The guide is divided into chapters according to the six books of *The Lord of the Rings*, and I would recommend reading each book of Tolkien's first, before turning to the relevant chapter in the reader's guide. In this reader's guide, I walk through each chapter of Tolkien's tale, highlighting certain key aspects of the narrative, sharing relevant backstory from the broader legendarium of Middle-earth, and offering translations of passages and some of the names composed in Tolkien's invented languages. Every chapter title of *The Lord of the Rings* is noted in bold typeface in the guide, so that each chapter can also be referenced easily.

Throughout the reader's guide I have included interludes that reflect on a variety of themes connected to Tolkien's biography and process of writing, with particular emphasis on the imagination. These interludes are drawn from the research I conducted for my doctoral dissertation, and are connected to the larger thesis presented in my work *The Back of Beyond: The Red Books of C.G. Jung and J.R.R. Tolkien*. Thus, both implicitly and explicitly throughout this text I draw on certain key concepts from Jungian analytical psychology, and from my own scholarly background which is greatly informed by depth psychology and archetypal studies.

I use the term "imaginal" throughout the guide to refer to activities of the imagination that express a certain quality of truth and reality. The particular definition of this word comes from Henry Corbin, who distinguished between the "imaginary," or that which is just "made up," and the "imaginal," which can be understood as "the object of imaginative or imagining perception."[1] The imaginal realm, based upon this definition, is a world that is not simply made up or invented, but rather discovered through imagining perception or active imagination.

The imaginal realm can be understood as being essentially synonymous with the realm Tolkien called Faërie. Tolkien wrote about the land of Faërie many times, perhaps most prominently in his essay "On Fairy-Stories," and in his short story, *Smith of Wootton Major*. In a passage cut from the original publication of "On Fairy-Stories," Tolkien offers the following illustration of Faërie:

---

[1] Henry Corbin, "Mundus Imaginalis, or The Imaginary and the Imaginal," trans. Ruth Horine, *Spring: An Annual of Archetypal Psychology and Jungian Thought* (1972): 10.

The Land of Fairy Story is wide and deep and high . . . its seas are shoreless and its stars uncounted, its beauty an enchantment and its peril ever-present; both joy and sorrow are poignant as a sword. In that land a man may (perhaps) count himself fortunate to have wandered, but its very mystery and wealth make dumb the traveller who would report. And while he is there it is dangerous for him to ask too many questions, lest the gates be shut and the keys be lost. The fairy gold (too often) turns to withered leaves when it is brought away. All that I can ask is that you, knowing all these things, will receive my withered leaves, as a token at least that my hand once held a little of the gold.[2]

Faërie, or the imaginal realm, is a domain that does not exist in a physical location, but that does not mean it is a place that does not exist at all, or is only made up or unreal. When you close your eyes, or when you read a story, images naturally arise. Where do these images come from? They exist in the imaginal realm, and we access them through the faculty of the imagination. Sometimes these images are fleeting, blurry, or ephemeral, and they are hard to grasp. But sometimes they can be fully immersive, what some call visions or visionary

---

2 J. R. R. Tolkien, *On Fairy-Stories*, "Manuscript B," ed. Verlyn Flieger and Douglas A. Anderson, (London: HarperCollins, 2014), 207.

experiences. We can even actively participate in them if we cultivate the practice or the discipline. This is what C.G. Jung called "active imagination": a meditation with images that arise from the unconscious.[3]

The book you hold in your hands is centered upon the imagination of the reader, with the intention of focusing upon and celebrating the images that arise internally when one reads *The Lord of the Rings*. J.R.R. Tolkien was a master at the craft of shaping the images and stories that arise through the imagination, and he is a skilled yet humble guide through the regions of the imaginal realm that he called Middle-earth. Included in this guide are several exquisite images drawn by the artist Arik Roper, who has made illustrations that seek to coax forward your own visions of Tolkien's story, rather than overlaying them with his own concrete artistic interpretations. I believe this is how Tolkien would have wanted such illustrations to be: fading into ephemerality at the edges, leading one's own imagination hither to unseen vistas and scenes.

If you have never read *The Lord of the Rings* before, let me say this to you: you are so lucky because now

---

[3] C.G. Jung, "The Concept of the Collective Unconscious," in *The Portable Jung*, ed. Joseph Campbell, trans. R.F.C. Hull, (New York: Penguin, 1976), 67.

an extraordinary new adventure awaits you. If this is your first time entering the world of Middle-earth, I have two pieces of advice. First, if you have not read *The Hobbit*, I would suggest that you consider reading it, although it is not absolutely essential reading before undertaking *The Lord of the Rings*. *The Hobbit* is a book written for children, while *The Lord of the Rings* is intended for an adult audience. Some find it difficult to start *The Hobbit* because it is a children's story, and if reading this book is hindering you starting *The Lord of the Rings* then I would suggest skipping it for now (you may find yourself called to read it afterwards, and may be surprised at the joy of the experience). The most essential chapter of *The Hobbit* is chapter five, "Riddles in the Dark." That chapter contains the most important information for the unfolding of *The Lord of the Rings*.

The second piece of advice regards beginning reading *The Lord of the Rings* itself: Tolkien wrote a "Foreword to the Second Edition" and a "Prologue," and if this is your first time reading this book I would suggest skipping these two sections until after you have finished the tale. Tolkien makes references to events that unfold in the narrative itself, which can make reading these sections a somewhat confusing experience. I would not want you to get bogged down in names and details before they hold any essential meaning for you. These two sections are deliciously interesting once you have finished the full story, and want to know more about Middle-earth and how this book came to be in your hands. So if this is your first time stepping across the threshold into the imaginal realm of Middle-earth, I would suggest not lingering at the doorstep but plunging directly into the first chapter, "A Long-Expected Party."

B.T.
July 29, 2019
Nevada City, California

A Biographical Introduction

WHEN PROFESSOR J.R.R. TOLKIEN of Oxford, England set out to write *The Lord of the Rings*, he did not know he would end up writing one of the most beloved works of literature of the twentieth century. Indeed, he did not know of hobbits or the King of Gondor, or even of Mount Doom. But he did know about Elves, and Middle-earth, the endless Sea, and the far shores of Faërie. He knew he wanted to write poems and tell stories that had a particular "quality of strangeness and wonder," that would bring "the satisfaction of certain primordial human desires," the desire "to survey the depths of space and time" and "hold communion with other living things."[1] And this he did, penning thousands of pages that came to tell the many stories of Middle-earth.

Over the course of his lifetime, Tolkien published the books *The Hobbit* and *The Lord of the Rings*, the short stories *Leaf by Niggle*, *Farmer Giles of Ham*, and *Smith of*

---

1 Tolkien, *On Fairy-Stories*, 34–35.

Wootton Major, and the book of poetry *The Adventures of Tom Bombadil and Other Verses from the Red Book*. He translated the medieval English poems *Sir Gawain and the Green Knight*, *Pearl*, and *Sir Orfeo*, and wrote scholarly papers on *Beowulf* and the *Ancrene Wisse*. But, except for the twelve long years dedicated to the composition of his masterwork, *The Lord of the Rings*, Tolkien's primary creative occupation was writing and re-writing the cosmogonic myths and epic tales of *The Silmarillion*, a book never published in his lifetime. Indeed, when he passed away in 1973, he left behind him "the serried ranks of box files that contained ... like beads without a string, the raw material of 'The Silmarillion.'"[2] As his publisher Rayner Unwin said: "although over the years some authors have written at greater length, few if any have left behind a more purposeful yet inchoate creative complexity than Tolkien."[3] But, thanks to the decades-long effort of Tolkien's son Christopher, the world can now read these pages, published as a compact narrative in *The Silmarillion*, and in the vast drafts and retellings found in *Unfinished Tales* and the twelve

---

2 Rayner Unwin, "Early Days of Elder Days," in *Tolkien's Legendarium: Essays on The History of Middle-Earth*, ed. Verlyn Flieger and Carl F. Hostetter, (Westport, CT: Greenwood Press, 2000), 247.

3 Unwin, "Early Days of Elder Days," 6.

volumes of *The History of Middle-Earth*. Indeed, we now have available to us Tolkien's "Great Tales," the three primary narratives of the First Age of Middle-earth, each published as individual volumes: *The Children of Húrin*, *Beren and Lúthien*, and *The Fall of Gondolin*.

Who knows what form *The Silmarillion* may have taken if Tolkien had given it the same level of perfectionist revisioning that he gave *The Lord of the Rings*. But perhaps that is not how the tales of Middle-earth were meant to be told. Perhaps they were meant to be received in the way the mythologies of our own world have been received: with overlapping narratives and changing names, some stories drawn with great detail in both poetry and prose, others sketched as tales to be glimpsed in the background. Exploring the world of Middle-earth can be like crossing a threshold into another realm, losing sight even of the pages in one's hands, as far landscapes and poignant beauties pierce to the depths of one's experience.

As his philological collaborator Simone D'Ardenne writes: "Tolkien's personality was so rich, so diverse, so vast and so elusive" that to paint any portrait of his life will inherently be inadequate.[4] Although born in

---

4 Simone D'Ardenne, "The Man and Scholar," in *J.R.R. Tolkien, Scholar and Storyteller: Essays in Memoriam*, ed. Mary Salu and

South Africa in 1892, Tolkien spent the majority of his life in England, only going to the European continent a few times, or occasionally across the water to Ireland. But this does not mean he was untraveled. Tolkien arguably explored more distant lands than many, but they are lands only found in the imagination.

When he was three years old, the young Ronald Tolkien sailed to England with his mother Mabel Suffield and younger brother Hilary to visit his mother's family. While they were there, just after Tolkien had turned four years old, his father Arthur Tolkien was taken suddenly ill and died. None of the family would ever return to South Africa again, and Tolkien would grow up without knowing his father. This is worth keeping in mind when we see how many figures in *The Lord of the Rings* and in Tolkien's other writings are orphans, or whose fathers or mothers die young. Perhaps the most significant of these orphans is Frodo, who is at the heart of this tale. Both his parents died when he was young, and it was his older cousin Bilbo who adopted him as heir. Likewise, the father of Aragorn—or Strider as he is first known—died when he was only two years old.

Tolkien's mother Mabel raised her two sons in a cottage in the English countryside, in a place called

---

Robert T. Farrell, (Ithaca, NY: Cornell UP, 1979), 33.

Sarehole. This landscape would significantly shape Tolkien's imagination, and we can see it reflected in the Shire, the idyllic pastoral homeland of the hobbits where both *The Hobbit* and *The Fellowship of the Ring* begin. Mabel gave Tolkien his first taste of foreign languages, and awakened in him a passion for fairy-story and myth.[5] Mabel taught her son Latin, French, and German, but he would go on to learn nineteen languages, many of them no longer spoken, such as Gothic, Old Icelandic, and Anglo-Saxon.[6] Tolkien had a skill for philology that once led his close friend C.S. Lewis to say: "He had been inside language."[7] From childhood Tolkien began inventing his own languages—a passion or "secret vice" he worked at throughout his life.[8] *The Lord of the Rings* contains quotes and passages from fourteen of Tolkien's invented languages.[9]

---

5 Philip Zaleski and Carol Zaleski, *The Fellowship: The Literary Lives of the Inklings* (New York: Farrar, Straus and Giroux, 2015), 17.

6 Ruth S. Noel, *The Languages of Tolkien's Middle-Earth* (Boston, MA: Houghton Mifflin, 1974), 3–4.

7 C.S. Lewis, "Professor J.R.R. Tolkien: Creator of Hobbits and Inventor of a New Mythology" in *J.R.R. Tolkien, Scholar and Storyteller: Essays in Memoriam*, ed. Mary Salu and Robert T. Farrell, (Ithaca, NY: Cornell UP, 1979), 12.

8 J.R.R. Tolkien, "A Secret Vice," in *The Monsters and the Critics*, ed. Christopher Tolkien, (London: HarperCollins, 2006), 198.

9 Noel, *The Languages of Tolkien's Middle-Earth*, 6.

Perhaps the most significant gift Mabel bestowed on her young son was his faith, a commitment to Roman Catholicism that would last a lifetime. In June 1900, when Tolkien was eight years old, Mabel and her sister May Incledon joined the Catholic Church.[10] The response of Mabel's Anglican family was to reject her along with her faith. They cut off much-needed financial support, as well as any relational connection. Her sister's husband forced May to renounce her new faith, and Mabel found herself more alone in the world than when her husband had died. Over the next four years Mabel's health rapidly deteriorated with the onset of diabetes, and in November 1904 she passed away. She left her two orphaned sons in the care of Father Francis Morgan, who was a priest of Spanish heritage born the same year as Tolkien's father.[11] Tolkien viewed his mother as a martyr to her faith, and his admiration for her echoed through all the years of his life. He said of her: "she was a gifted lady of great beauty and wit, greatly stricken by God with grief and suffering, who died in youth of a disease hastened by persecution of her faith."[12]

---

10 Zaleski and Zaleski, *The Fellowship: The Literary Lives of the Inklings*, 19.

11 Raymond Edwards, *Tolkien* (London: Robert Hale, 2014), 27.

12 J. R. R. Tolkien, *The Letters of J. R. R. Tolkien*, eds. Humphrey Carpenter & Christopher Tolkien (New York: Houghton Mifflin, 2000), 54.

Friendship played a crucial role in Tolkien's life, perhaps in part because of the early loss of his parents. As his close friend C. S. Lewis once remarked: "He was a man of 'cronies' rather than of general society and was always best after midnight . . . and in some small circle of intimates where the tone was at once Bohemian, literary, and Christian."[13] Two fellowships were central to Tolkien's life, one formed in youth, the other later in adulthood. The first group was named the Tea Club and Barrovian Society, referred to simply as the TCBS, and it had its beginnings in the library of King Edward's School, where Tolkien received his primary education before entering Exeter College, Oxford. The latter group was the Inklings, the Oxford literary group that gathered during the 1930s and 1940s in C. S. Lewis's Magdalen College rooms. As one of its members remarked, the Inklings were "a circle of instigators, almost incendiaries, meeting to urge one another on in the task of redirecting the whole current of contemporary art and life."[14] The group included Lewis's brother Warnie, the anthroposophist and philosopher Owen Barfield, and the poet and novelist Charles Williams

---

13 Lewis, "Professor J. R. R. Tolkien," 15.
14 John Barrington Wain, *Sprightly Running: Part of an Autobiography* (New York: St. Martin's, 1962), 181.

among several others, and eventually included Tolkien's third son, Christopher. Although the group never had an official membership, the Lewis brothers and Tolkien were always at the core.

Tolkien began writing *The Lord of the Rings* in 1937, following the successful publication of his children's book, *The Hobbit*. His publisher, Allen and Unwin, said the public was clamoring for more on hobbits, and asked Tolkien if he would be interested in writing another story. At first Tolkien decided to submit some materials he had already written. He included his tales from the First Age of Middle-earth, tales that would be published much later as *The Silmarillion*. These poems and tales of the First Age had been Tolkien's primary creative focus for over two decades already, but it had largely been a private matter.

Tolkien wrote the first poem of Middle-earth in 1914, while he was still a student at Oxford. The poem was called "The Voyage of Éarendel the Evening Star." Here is the first verse:

> *Éarendel sprang up from the Ocean's cup*
> *In the gloom of the mid-world's rim;*
> *From the door of Night as a ray of light*
> *Leapt over the twilight brim,*
> *And launching his bark like a silver spark*

From the golden-fading sand
Down the sunlit breath of Day's fiery death
He sped from Westerland.[15]

But who is Éarendel? Tolkien read the name Éarendel for the first time in 1913, in an Anglo-Saxon verse called *Crist*, composed by the poet Cynewulf. There were two lines that particularly stood out to him:

Eala Éarendel engla beorhtast
ofer middangeard monnum sended.

Hail Éarendel, brightest of angels
above the middle-earth sent unto men.[16]

Long afterwards, Tolkien wrote: "I felt a curious thrill as if something had stirred in me, half wakened from sleep. There was something very remote and strange and beautiful behind those words, if I could grasp it,

---

15 J.R.R. Tolkien, "The Tale of Eärendel," in *The History of Middle-Earth: The Book of Lost Tales*, Part II, vol. 2, ed. Christopher Tolkien, (New York: Houghton Mifflin, 2010), 268.

16 Humphrey Carpenter, *J.R.R. Tolkien: A Biography*, 72; Tolkien, "The Notion Club Papers," in *The History of Middle-Earth: Sauron Defeated*, vol. 9, ed. Christopher Tolkien, (New York: Houghton Mifflin, 2010), 236.

far beyond ancient English."[17] Not only is the name Éarendel in these lines, but the name of the land where all these stories take place: *middangeard*, or Middle-earth.

Tolkien showed "The Voyage of Éarendel" to his close friend Geoffrey Bache Smith, who was a fellow member of the TCBS, Tolkien's schoolboy fellowship. After reading it, Smith asked what the poem was really about. Tolkien gave an unusual response: "I don't know. I'll try to find out."[18] He would later maintain this sense of discovery that came with all his stories: that he was not merely making them up, but rather he was finding out "what really happened."[19]

Tolkien would describe his process of writing stories as one of uncovering something that already had, to a certain degree, an objective existence. In speaking about his stories, he once said: "I have long ceased to *invent* ... I wait till I seem to know what really happened. Or till it writes itself."[20] He claimed that the stories "arose in my mind as 'given' things, and as they came, separately, so too the links grew. ... Always I had the sense of recording what was already 'there,'

---

17 Carpenter, *Tolkien: A Biography*, 72.
18 Carpenter, *Tolkien: A Biography*, 83.
19 Tolkien, *Letters*, 212.
20 Tolkien, *Letters*, 231.

somewhere: not of 'inventing.'"[21] Both the separate stories, and the larger narrative whole of the legendarium, came to Tolkien as given—a gift bestowed from somewhere beyond his own individual being. Tolkien once stated in a letter to his son Christopher, "the thing seems to write itself once I get going, as if the truth comes out then, only imperfectly glimpsed in the preliminary sketch."[22] When Tolkien discussed *The Lord of the Rings*, or his other stories of Middle-earth, he spoke about it not as a work of fiction but rather as a chronicle of actual events. He considered himself not as the author of his stories, but rather a historian and a translator of a record already in existence.[23]

Tolkien's tales of Middle-earth began with the poem "The Voyage of Éarendel," but these soon began to expand, especially after he joined Kitchener's Army in the First World War, known then as the Great War. Tolkien wrote the first of what he would come to call the Great Tales in 1916. This tale was "The Fall of Gondolin." Soon after, in 1917 Tolkien wrote "The Tale of Tinúviel," which would someday become *Beren and Lúthien*. He composed "Turambar and the Foalókë"

---

21 Tolkien, *Letters*, 145.

22 Tolkien, *Letters*, 104.

23 Carpenter, *Tolkien: A Biography*, 12.

during this period, which would come to be called "Of Túrin Turambar" and also *The Children of Húrin*. In 1919 Tolkien also wrote a creation myth that he called "The Music of the Ainur." He would come to call this cosmogonic myth the *Ainulindalë*, which means "The Music of the Ainur" in Elvish.

Tolkien recast the "The Tale of Tinúviel" and "The Children of Húrin" in the 1920s as two epic poems, neither of which he finished. But it was all of these tales, in poetry and prose, and several other half-finished stories as well, that Tolkien submitted to his publisher Allen and Unwin in 1937, when they asked if he had any more material about hobbits. Needless to say, these somber Elvish histories did not appeal to the publisher, and the reader who judged the material stated that the many unusual names were "eye-splitting."[24] Tolkien was extraordinarily disappointed by the rejection, but agreed to try to write more about hobbits, although he felt to himself that he had said everything he might say about them in Bilbo Baggins' tale, *The Hobbit: Or There and Back Again*. It is remarkable to think that now publishers are eager to print anything Tolkien ever wrote, any scrap of unfinished narrative or poetry, as well as showing exhibits of his sketches and half-finished

---

24 Carpenter, *Tolkien: A Biography*, 188.

working maps, alongside his more completed artwork. I wonder what Tolkien would have made of it, especially Tolkien in 1937 when he was resigning himself to the idea that his beloved *Silmarillion* might never be published. Thus, instead of having *The Silmarillion* published in the 1930s, Tolkien began writing a new tale, one that would take him on an unforeseen adventure.

To this adventure we now turn, and alongside Tolkien begin to walk the road that leads through Middle-earth. Thus, we now begin our journey to the imaginal realm. The story begins in autumn. Autumn is the time of wanderings, of passing between realms. The Elves take the road westward in autumn. Frodo feels the call to adventure in autumn. Bilbo's and Frodo's birthdays are at the fall equinox, on September 22. *The Lord of the Rings* tells of the ending of the Third Age, the passing of an era. It is a time of fall. The leaves wither and fall to the ground, but new life sleeps below the Earth.

Bag End

1

The Fellowship of the Ring – *Book I*
From Hobbiton to Rivendell

*T*HE LORD OF THE RINGS—which Tolkien at first titled simply *The New Hobbit*—begins in a similar manner as *The Hobbit*. Instead of "An Unexpected Party," in which thirteen dwarves and the wizard Gandalf show up on Bilbo Baggins' doorstep at Bag End, *The Lord of the Rings* begins with **"A Long-Expected Party."** We find ourselves in the humble village of Hobbiton, nestled safely in the Shire. The opening chapter is fairly light-hearted, and echoes the style of *The Hobbit* in a number of ways. We are deep in the world and culture of the hobbits, saturated in descriptions of the gossip, the food and drink, the family ties and connections, and the little harmless quarrels.

The key moment in this opening chapter is Bilbo's speech under the Party Tree. He refers to "ancient history," speaking about one of his adventures with the dwarves that took place during *The Hobbit*.[1] And then

---

1 J.R.R. Tolkien, *The Lord of the Rings: The Fellowship of the Ring* (New York: Houghton Mifflin, 2014), I, i, 30.

he makes the "Announcement": that he is going to leave, that this is the end. And then he vanishes. With the help of the little magic ring he obtained during his travels, Bilbo disappears, and that startling act leads to the intriguing and telling conversation with Gandalf inside Bag End. We see the grip the Ring already has on Bilbo, how it shifts him into anger and possessiveness. We learn that the whole purpose of the enormous birthday party was simply to make it easier for Bilbo to give the Ring to Frodo, as he was giving away so much else that day. But in the end the parting is not easier. We see the swift change of emotions when he finally lets go of the Ring: a spasm of anger, but then relief and a laugh. Something has passed through him.

The second chapter, **"The Shadow of the Past,"** covers a great span of time—seventeen years between the birthday party and the main events of this chapter. During that time Frodo has grown older, although not much in appearance. He often wanders the Shire, sometimes under starlight, and is rumored to at times visit with the Elves. Clearly, Frodo is not a usual hobbit. Notice that it is in autumn that Frodo feels the call of the wild lands, and that he sees strange visions of unknown mountains in his dreams. Tolkien wrote this second chapter much later, when he had more of a sense of how the story was unfolding, but placed it here near the beginning because of the important historical information it contains. At first it may be challenging to take in everything revealed in this chapter, because many of the names are unfamiliar and it is so early in the story. But this is a chapter worth referencing and coming back to as you progress through the story. I think of it as one of the research chapters, or historical chapters. There are a few more of these later in the story, which I will mention as we go along. In this second chapter, we hear certain important names for the first time: the Enemy or the Dark Lord, whose name is Sauron, and we hear of his Land of Mordor and the Dark Tower at its center. As is peripherally covered in *The Hobbit*, there existed an evil power in Mirkwood that was driven forth by the White Council. Who are the White Council? You will meet many of the members later on, but I can say now it includes Gandalf, Saruman, Elrond, and Galadriel. Perhaps only one or two of these names is familiar at this stage in the story, but we will encounter them later. These are the figures who work for good in the world, for freedom, for diversity, for the flourishing of life and beauty.

We also receive our first close glimpse of Samwise Gamgee in this chapter. The name "Samwise" translates as "half-wit," something to keep in mind.[2] But is

---

2 Tolkien, *Letters*, 83.

he really a half-wit? Sam argues with the skeptic Ted Sandyman about the strange rumors that the hobbits have been hearing—rumors of Elves passing into the West, greater numbers of Dwarves on the road East, and dark whispers of the Enemy stirring in Mordor—and Sam claims that there are more to tales and stories than is often credited. We can hear Tolkien's own voice speaking through Sam here, telling us of the hidden truth at the heart of fairy-tales, legends, and myths. Sam even mentions a walking tree—something to remember for when we come to *The Two Towers*.

When Gandalf finally returns to the Shire, after much time away and only a few visits in those seventeen years, he begins to tell Frodo about the Ring. We dip here into the ancient history of Middle-earth. Gandalf speaks about Eregion, a land that was once inhabited by Elves. If you look at the map of Middle-earth, you can see that Eregion lies to the west of the Misty Mountains. In Eregion, Elven-smiths made the Great Rings and, as the poem says, three were for the Elves, seven for the Dwarves, Nine for Men, and One that was made not by the Elves but by Sauron. Sauron learned the secrets of the Elves' ring lore, and made his own Ruling Ring to master all the others. What is important to know is that the Three Rings of the Elves are bound to the One, but are not under its power—they are hidden, in the hands of three keepers. Who are these three keepers? You will find out, one by one.

The history of how the One Ring came into Bilbo's hands is a long one, and Gandalf omits many parts of the story. At this stage in the narrative this would be far too much information. He chooses to mention the Last Alliance between Men and Elves, a military alliance which took place at the end of the Second Age of Middle-earth. The high king of the Elves in Middle-earth at this time was named Gil-galad, which means "starlight." And the king of the Men of Westernesse was Elendil, which means "elf-friend." Who are the Men of Westernesse? You will hear this name mentioned sporadically throughout the tale. Westernesse is also called Númenor, and it was a great island civilization, far to the west of Middle-earth. Due to great arrogance and betrayal, this island was drowned during the Second Age of Middle-earth, and it sank beneath the waves of the sea and only those called the Faithful escaped. The island was called the Downfallen, which translates into Elvish as Atalantë. Does this not sound something like Atlantis? An island in the sea, home to a great civilization, has been an archetypal image at the heart of numerous mythologies worldwide, and an image that carried particular significance for Tolkien, as will be explored later.

Elendil was the leader of the Faithful, and it was his son Isildur who later cut the Ring from the Dark Lord Sauron's hand, leading to Sauron's downfall for several thousand years. Two important elements ought to be emphasized here: after the war of the Last Alliance, Isildur first returned to the southern kingdom of Gondor and left a record about the Ring, describing it in close detail. Only after this did he travel north, in order to return to his own kingdom, Arnor, and to reunite with his youngest son who had been left in Rivendell with Elrond. If you have read *The Hobbit*, you have been to Rivendell and met Elrond. The entire trajectory of Book I of *The Lord of the Rings* is leading towards Rivendell. This is an ancient place, present in stories not only from the Third Age of Middle-earth—during which *The Lord of the Rings* takes place—but the Second Age as well.

As Isildur was returning home, he and his company were waylaid by orcs. He tried to escape by putting on the Ring and swimming invisibly across the river, but the Ring betrayed him and slipped off his finger and sank to the bottom of the Great River. On the map you can see the Great River, also called the Anduin, running to the east of the Misty Mountains down the whole length of Middle-earth. When the Ring abandoned Isildur he was rendered visible, and orcs slew him with arrows. These events all take place more than two thousand years before the events in *The Lord of the Rings*.

Gandalf next tells the remarkable tale that he reconstructed from his encounter with the creature Gollum. We first met Gollum in the chapter "Riddles in the Dark" in *The Hobbit*. Gollum is an unforgettable figure, utterly unique in literature and perhaps in imagination. There is an audio recording available of J.R.R. Tolkien reading this chapter of "Riddles in the Dark" aloud, and if you have not heard it I recommend it highly.[3] No one can express Gollum's voice better than Tolkien himself.

Several moments of pure wisdom glimmer in this chapter. Gandalf speaks of the pity that Bilbo felt for Gollum, leading to his choice not kill Gollum when he had a chance. Gandalf says: "Many that live deserve death. And some that die deserve life. Can you give it to them? Then do not be too eager to deal out death in judgement. For even the very wise cannot see all ends."[4] Gandalf knows his limitations. Archetypally, he is the senex, but he is also the fool. He is the trickster and the wise old man.

---

[3] See J.R.R. Tolkien reads "Riddles in the Dark" from *The Hobbit*: https://www.youtube.com/watch?v=bAoOgL8omsw&t=52s. [last accessed 29 July 2009]

[4] Tolkien, *The Fellowship of the Ring*, I, ii, 58.

This chapter contains perhaps my favorite line from the entire book, if it is possible to choose just one. It follows when Frodo says: "I wish it need not have happened in my time."[5] How many of us have also felt that? How many of us feel that in our current era, as the days seem to darken around us? But listen to how Gandalf responds: "'So do I,' said Gandalf, 'and so do all who live to see such times. But that is not for them to decide. All we have to decide is what to do with the time that is given us.'"[6] *All we have to decide is what to do with the time that is given us.* We can remember that insight, that we always have that choice to decide what to do with the gift of the time we do have.

After this historical chapter, the adventure at last begins. In some ways it is a slow beginning, with the three chapters "Three is Company," "A Shortcut to Mushrooms," and "A Conspiracy Unmasked" taking the same meandering time that the hobbits are. Yet there is a sinister quality in the air. When Tolkien was writing these chapters, he did not know how this tale was meant to unfold. He was taking each step forward with as little knowing as Frodo, Sam, and Pippin as they walk across the Shire. While Tolkien was writing,

---

5 Tolkien, *The Fellowship of the Ring*, I, ii, 50.
6 Tolkien, *The Fellowship of the Ring*, I, ii, 50.

a horseman dressed in black appeared on the road of his imagination. Tolkien himself did not know who this was. He suspected perhaps it was Gandalf, but he could not be sure. Tolkien was not simply inventing or making his stories up, he was discovering them as they unfolded. He shaped with great art and much editing what came through, but the primary visions in the tale were springing directly from the imaginal realm. When he realized that the Black Rider was not Gandalf, he suddenly had to come to terms with this story no longer being a children's book as *The Hobbit* had been. This new narrative had taken on a life of its own.

In the third chapter, "**Three is Company**," we meet Gildor and his company of High Elves. There are many kinds of Elves in Middle-earth, but the High Elves are those who lived for a time in the Undying Lands, the immortal realm across the Great Sea to the West. They are called the Noldor. Many of the most prominent or important Elves we meet are of the Noldor, who see themselves as exiles in Middle-earth. Why they are exiles is a long story from the First Age, which is at the heart of *The Silmarillion*. But for now we simply need to know these are powerful and wise Elves, who have seen the light of the Blessed Realm.

The Elves sing to Elbereth, whose name is also Gilthoniel. She is one of the Valar, one of the pantheon of Powers or Gods of the world. She has many names: Varda, Elbereth, Gilthoniel, Eléntari, Tintallë. Her name itself is sacred. Elbereth means "star queen," and Gilthoniel means "star kindler." You will hear her name again and again, at significant moments, spoken almost like a prayer.

Gildor names Frodo "Elf-friend," which is a significant name bestowed upon certain mortals in these tales.[7] Each time you hear the name Elf-friend, it is worth paying attention. There is a lineage of Elf-friends that stretches back into the stories of the First Age as told in *The Silmarillion*, and even to the earliest tales Tolkien ever wrote of Middle-earth, recorded in *The Book of Lost Tales*. They are figures set apart, for having a trustworthy relationship to the Elves, and often for being witnesses to the myths and legends of the Eldar.[8] In *The Book of Lost Tales*, these stories are told to a wandering mariner who finds an island of the Elves by chance. The mariner's name was Eriol—meaning "one who dreams alone"—but in later revisions Tolkien changed his name to Ælfwine, which translates as

---

7 Tolkien, *The Fellowship of the Ring*, I, iii, 79.
8 For an essay exploring the significance of the phrase "Elf-friend," see Verlyn Flieger, "The Footsteps of Ælfwine," in *Green Suns and Faërie: Essays on J. R. R. Tolkien* (Kent, OH: The Kent State UP, 2012), 74–88.

"Elf-friend." Names with this meaning still exist today. For example, the Anglo-Saxon name Alfred can be translated as "Elf-friend." The name Godwin can be translated as "God-friend." As Tolkien discusses in his unfinished story *The Notion Club Papers*, there must be some reason that several names from the medieval era carry references to Elves or to the gods. Tolkien embedded his curiosity around these names into his stories, and when we hear the name "Elf-friend" we can know it refers to one who traverses between worlds, a mortal who has been given a glimpse of the immortal world of the Elves.

At the beginning of the fourth chapter, **"A Shortcut to Mushrooms,"** Sam speaks of his conversation with the Elves, and then he reflects to himself about his own role in this journey. Sam says he can see ahead, and can see they will take a long road into darkness. He knows he cannot turn back. Is this really a half-wit speaking? Sam is a hobbit with vision, who can perhaps see into the unfolding future. He knows he has something to do before the end.

In the fifth chapter, **"A Conspiracy Unmasked,"** we hear how the three hobbits who will accompany Frodo on his journey have been tracking his movements and his plans. Significantly, we learn that Merry is the only person besides Frodo to have glimpsed Bilbo's secret book. The book he is referring to is Bilbo's red diary in which he recorded his adventures with the dwarves. At this point, the book is essentially the equivalent story told in *The Hobbit*. But someday this book will contain the full tale of *The Lord of the Rings*, and it will be known as *The Red Book of Westmarch*. Each mention of *The Red Book* is significant, because it is the tale referring to itself, to the means through which we now have a copy of the story in our own hands. Tolkien is grounding his tale in history, in a book tradition.[9]

In some ways, the adventure does not really begin until chapter six, **"The Old Forest."** Here the four hobbits cross the threshold of the Shire, marked by the great Hedge, and enter into all that lies outside. The true journey has begun—and little seems to go right. Traveling through the Old Forest is slow-going, and we can feel as tangled and hampered as the hobbits. An interesting tension is present here too, between the will of the hobbits and the will of the forest. Tolkien had a deep love and respect for trees, yet whose side are we meant to be on when we hear of the forest encroaching upon the Hedge, or of Old Man Willow entrapping

---

[9] For more on how *The Red Book of Westmarch* connects *The Lord of the Rings* to the medieval book tradition, see Verlyn Flieger, "Tolkien and the Idea of the Book," in *Green Suns and Faërie: Essays on J. R. R. Tolkien*, 41–53.

Pippin and Merry in his bark? We tend to side with the hobbits, and yet we can see there is more than a polarity between good and evil in this tale. There are different desires, and they do not always align.[10]

In this chapter we also encounter Tom Bombadil, who is an anomaly in the world of Middle-earth. Who is he? He is called oldest and fatherless. In the seventh chapter, **"In the House of Tom Bombadil,"** Goldberry says of Bombadil that "He is."[11] This seems almost to echo the biblical phrase spoken by God: "I Am Who Am." But I do not believe Tolkien is indicating that Tom Bombadil is God here, by any means. He simply *is*, and he does not fit into the tightly woven world that Tolkien illuminated. Everything fits, everything is consistent in that world. Middle-earth has the "inner consistency of reality" of which Tolkien speaks in his essay "On Fairy-Stories."[12] But Tom Bombadil stands apart; he is altogether different. I have wondered if Bombadil represents Tolkien himself in some way. Tom Bombadil in fact far pre-existed *The Lord of the Rings*, and was

---

10 For more on the ambiguity of sides in ecological conflict, see Verlyn Flieger, "Taking the Part of the Trees: Eco-conflict in Middle-earth," in *Green Suns and Faërie: Essays on J.R.R. Tolkien*, 262–74.

11 Tolkien, *The Fellowship of the Ring*, I, vii, 122.

12 Tolkien, *On Fairy-Stories*, 59.

a figure in several poems Tolkien wrote, one of which was called "The Adventures of Tom Bombadil." The poem was eventually published in 1962 alongside a collection of Tolkien's other poems under the title *The Adventures of Tom Bombadil and Other Verses from the Red Book*.

When we come to the house of Tom Bombadil we meet Goldberry, who is the daughter of the River. She seems Elf-like, but not quite so. They are an odd couple, this funny small man and this elegant, exquisite woman. They both seem to be nature spirits, but of a rather different order. They are a *syzygy*, to use a Gnostic term, a pairing of opposites that make a coniunctio, a complete archetypal whole.

In the home of Goldberry and Tom, Frodo has two significant dreams. In the first, he sees a man upon a pinnacle of stone, in the midst of a plain surrounded by a ring of hills. The figure has white hair and a staff. Does that sound familiar? An eagle flies down and bears the man away. What does this dream portend? The second dream takes place at the opening of chapter eight, "Fog on the Barrow-Downs." The dream is worth quoting in full:

> Frodo heard a sweet singing running in his mind: a song that seemed to come like a pale light behind

a grey rain-curtain, and growing stronger to turn the veil all to glass and silver, until at last it was rolled back, and a far green country opened before him under a swift sunrise.[13]

These two dreams are worth remembering. Dreams and visions have an important role to play in this narrative. Frodo also dreams of the Sea during his night at the little house in Crickhollow.[14] Tolkien takes seriously what dreams and visions portend.

When the hobbits depart and are ensnared in the barrow-downs, the first truly frightening episode of the story unfolds. This scene is chilling. But perhaps most interesting is Merry's experience. When he awakens after Bombadil frees them from the barrow, he makes a curious statement. He says: "Of course, I remember!... The men of Carn Dûm came on us at night, and we were worsted. Ah! the spear in my heart!"[15] What is happening here? Merry's consciousness seems to have fused with the consciousness of the dead man buried in the barrow. The phenomenon itself of what Merry experiences is fascinating: something like a

---

13 Tolkien, *The Fellowship of the Ring*, I, viii, 132.
14 Tolkien, *The Fellowship of the Ring*, I, v, 106.
15 Tolkien, *The Fellowship of the Ring*, I, viii, 140.

transferred memory, or a vision of a past life.[16] In this memory or vision we have a hint of the history of these barrow-downs. The men of Carn Dûm were in service to the Witch-King of Angmar in ages past, who is the chief servant of the Dark Lord Sauron. Bombadil also speaks of these men when he discusses the blades that were forged by the Men of Westernesse—the Men of Númenor—to fight against the Men of Carn Dûm. Furthermore, Bombadil speaks of the sons of forgotten kings, who go wandering in the wilderness, guarding against evil things. The hobbits do not know what he is talking about, yet they all experience a collective vision of a lineage of Men, each carrying a sword. The final figure has a star on his brow. This too is a significant image, although its meaning will only become clear with time.

We next arrive at the village of Bree, in the ninth chapter **"At the Sign of the Prancing Pony."** Of course, Gandalf is not here—and this is worrisome. But we do meet a most important figure: Strider. He has a whole chapter named to himself, chapter ten, **"Strider."** Tolkien once said of his writing process: "I met a lot of

---

16 For an essay exploring Merry's experience in the barrow, see Verlyn Flieger, "The Curious Incident of the Dream at the Barrow: Memory and Reincarnation in Middle-Earth," in *Green Suns and Faërie: Essays on J. R. R. Tolkien*, 89–101.

things on the way that astonished me. Tom Bombadil I knew already; but I had never been to Bree. Strider sitting in the corner at the inn was a shock, and I had no more idea who he was than had Frodo."[17] This man sitting in the shadows is a mystery, but a compelling one. *"All that is gold does not glitter."*[18] His true name is revealed here, but it means little to us at this point: "I am Aragorn, son of Arathorn; and if by life or death I can save you, I will."[19] And this is what he proves to do.

Strider guides the hobbits into the Wild, and in the eleventh chapter, "A Knife in the Dark," he does indeed save their lives. We learn more in this chapter about the old history of the North Kingdom of the Men of the West, and we also learn more about the realm of Angmar. We discover that Sam knows something of this history from Bilbo, when he sings of the High King Gil-galad and the Last Alliance of Elves and Men.

We also discover there is much more to Strider than at first meets the eye. He sings to the hobbits the tale of Tinúviel, which was one of the Great Tales that Tolkien first wrote in 1917. The story tells of a mortal man named Beren and the great love he shared with

---

17 Tolkien, *Letters*, 216–17.
18 Tolkien, *The Fellowship of the Ring*, I, x, 167.
19 Tolkien, *The Fellowship of the Ring*, I, x, 168.

an elf-woman named Lúthien Tinúviel. At first, theirs was a forbidden love. Beren sees Lúthien dancing in a forest grove and becomes enchanted with her beauty and her grace. This image of a woman dancing beneath the trees comes from Tolkien's own life, when in 1917 he saw his young wife Edith Bratt dancing amongst the hemlocks while he was on medical leave from the First World War.[20] He said of Edith: "She was (and she knew she was) my Lúthien."[21] Edith had grey eyes, and you may notice that every character of great significance in the legendarium of Middle-earth also has grey eyes. Edith was Tolkien's great love, but she also was his anima figure—to use a term from Jungian psychology—his Lúthien.[22] The two figures, human and archetypal, blended. J.R.R. Tolkien and his wife Edith are buried together under a single tombstone outside of Oxford, and inscribed upon the stone is the following:

Edith Mary Tolkien
1889-1971
Lúthien

---

20 John Garth, *Tolkien and the Great War: The Threshold of Middle-Earth* (New York: Houghton Mifflin, 2003), 238.

21 Tolkien, *Letters*, 420.

22 Lance S. Owens, personal communication, 29 October 2015.

And below that is also inscribed:

> JOHN RONALD REUEL TOLKIEN
> 1892-1973
> BEREN

The love between Beren and Lúthien is the core of almost all the stories of Middle-earth, and their bloodline descends through the two kindreds of Elves and Men. Their descendants are central figures in this tale, although I will wait to name who they are until we are further in the story. In the end Beren and Lúthien both die mortal deaths, leaving the circles of the world forever, rather than being parted by their fates as mortal man and immortal elf.

After the fateful escape from the attack by the Black Riders on Weathertop, we enter the final chapter of Book I, **"Flight to the Ford."** Frodo is slipping between worlds because of his wound from the Morgul blade, between the world of the living and the otherworld. Their travels at this point are extremely precarious. It seems a miracle when the hobbits and Strider encounter the elf Glorfindel, who has been searching for them. Glorfindel's greeting is in Elvish: *"Ai na vedui Dúnadan!*

Mae govannen!"[23] "Oh at last, Dúnadan," is the translation of what he says.[24] "Dúnadan" is a proper name, but it also means "Man of the West." *Mae govannen* means "well met," and is the Elvish way to say hello.

Book I closes with the chase to the ford, Frodo riding the elf-horse Asfaloth. *"Noro lim,"* Glorfindel says to the horse, which means "Ride on."[25] Frodo crosses the ford, and invokes the sacred name of Elbereth, as well as the name of Lúthien. He calls on these powerful female protectors in this moment of greatest need, and the river responds, waves of water overcoming and washing away the nine Black Riders. In these last moments Frodo has crossed almost entirely into the otherworld—he can perceive the wraiths, but he can also perceive Glorfindel in his true form: a shining figure of white light. Glorfindel is one of the High Elves who has seen the Blessed Realm. That sacred light Frodo can now perceive directly through his altered consciousness.

Thus, Book I comes to a close as Frodo loses consciousness by the river's edge and all is covered in darkness.

---

23 Tolkien, *The Fellowship of the Ring*, I, xii, 204.
24 Noel, *The Languages of Tolkien's Middle-Earth*, 36.
25 Tolkien, *The Fellowship of the Ring*, I, xii, 208; Noel, *The Languages of Tolkien's Middle-Earth*, 37.

Interlude

Sub-Creation: Tolkien's Philosophy of Imagination

BEFORE CONTINUING with the story in Book II, I wish first to explore J.R.R. Tolkien's own understanding of his creative process. Tolkien developed a theory of imagination that he called "Sub-creation" as a way to understand the origin and creation of his stories, which he explicated in his essay "On Fairy-Stories." Tolkien defines "Imagination" as "the faculty of conceiving images," and "the mental power of image-making."[1] Yet he points out that over time the term "Imagination" has come to mean something more than the faculty of image-making. The term carries a greater potency: "the power of giving to ideal creations the inner consistency of reality."[2] Tolkien is alluding to the English Romantic poet Samuel Taylor Coleridge, and his discussion of the primary and secondary imagination as expressed in Coleridge's book *Biographia Literaria*. Coleridge delineates the primary imagination from the secondary

---

1   Tolkien, *On Fairy-Stories*, 59.
2   Tolkien, *On Fairy-Stories*, 59.

imagination as a difference in degree, but not a difference in kind.

Coleridge defined the primary imagination as follows: "The primary Imagination I hold to be the living power and prime agent of all human perception, and as a repetition in the finite mind of the eternal act of creation in the infinite I AM."[3] Coleridge is saying that the primary imagination creates the world we perceive, and shapes our very perception of it. The primary imagination gives to "ideal creations the inner consistency of reality," as Tolkien puts it. The primary imagination is the source of all images, the wellspring of creativity.

In *Biographia Literaria* Coleridge also delineates the secondary imagination, which he considers to be an "echo" of the primary imagination. Coleridge says that the secondary imagination is "co-existing with the conscious will, yet still as identical with the primary in the *kind* of its agency, and differing only in *degree*, and in the *mode* of its operation. It dissolves, diffuses, dissipates, in order to recreate."[4] The secondary imagination is the creative will of the human being, which takes the primary source of images and shapes

---

3 Samuel Taylor Coleridge, *Biographia Literaria* (London: J.M. Dent & Co., 1906), 159–60.

4 Coleridge, *Biographia Literaria*, 159.

it into art, bringing forth new form. Tolkien's theory of sub-creation echoes Coleridge's definitions of the primary and secondary imagination, although it is important to note that Tolkien chooses different terms for his concepts. Sub-creation is essentially a process in two primary stages: the experience of images arising through the "Imagination," and then the "Art" of shaping those images into the final result. Tolkien calls the final result "Sub-creative Art."[5] The two stages are "Imagination" and then "Art," and the result is a "Sub-creation." Yet Tolkien wanted another word that could simultaneously encompass this "Sub-creative Art" and also what he called that "quality of strangeness and wonder in the Expression, derived from the Image."[6] For this word, a word that could encompass all those qualities, Tolkien chose the term "Fantasy."[7]

The word "Fantasy" has a wide range of meanings for Tolkien. From his perspective, Fantasy is "the making or glimpsing of Other-worlds."[8] Fantasy is both an activity and the result of that activity. Fantasy is the capacity to create, but also to perceive, an otherworld;

---

5   Tolkien, *On Fairy-Stories*, 59.
6   Tolkien, *On Fairy-Stories*, 60.
7   Tolkien, *On Fairy-Stories*, 60.
8   Tolkien, *On Fairy-Stories*, 55.

and it encompasses the full sensory experience of that otherworld. As Tolkien writes: "Fantasy is a natural human activity. It certainly does not destroy or even insult Reason; and it does not either blunt the appetite for, nor obscure the perception of, scientific verity."[9] Tolkien is careful to differentiate fantasy from dreaming, and to distinguish it also from delusion, hallucination, and mental disorders: "Fantasy is a rational not an irrational activity."[10] Fantasy requires conscious engagement and control by means of the human will. And, as I mentioned previously, fantasy is also the word Tolkien chose to encompass what he meant by "Sub-creative Art." Thus "Fantasy" is a noun, an adjective, and a verb in Tolkien's vocabulary, and encompasses the full experience of "making or glimpsing Other-worlds."

According to Tolkien, a successful sub-creator "makes a Secondary World which your mind can enter. Inside it, what he relates is 'true': it accords with the laws of that world. You therefore believe it, while you are, as it were, inside."[11] Tolkien calls this occurrence "Secondary Belief."[12] Secondary belief is what we experience

---

9 Tolkien, *On Fairy-Stories*, 65.
10 Tolkien, *On Fairy-Stories*, 60, n. 2.
11 Tolkien, *On Fairy-Stories*, 52.
12 Tolkien, *On Fairy-Stories*, 64.

when we read a great story, a story such as *The Lord of the Rings*. We are able to enter into the world of Middle-earth. When one enters a secondary world, and the inner laws of that world are consistent, it feels as though one is truly in that place, seeing the landscapes, hearing the people speaking and interacting with one another, and witnessing events unfold through one's internal sensory perceptions. A true secondary world echoes the primary world in its expression of reality.

From Tolkien's perspective, there is yet another level of secondary belief. When secondary belief reaches its most actualized form, then one experiences "Enchantment." Tolkien writes: "Enchantment produces a Secondary World into which both designer and spectator can enter, to the satisfaction of their senses while they are inside; but in its purity it is artistic in desire and purpose."[13] Enchantment allows one to be fully immersed in a secondary world, beyond any doubt in its reality. Enchantment is what Frodo experiences in the first chapter of Book II, in the Hall of Fire when he hears the Elvish music and visions begin to unfold before him.[14] He knows the story being told even though he does not understand all the Elvish words. That is

---

13 Tolkien, *On Fairy-Stories*, 64.
14 Tolkien, *The Fellowship of the Ring*, II, i, 227.

an experience of enchantment, or what Tolkien also at times calls a Faërian Drama.[15]

Tolkien only uses the term Faërian Drama in a few places, in the essay "On Fairy-Stories" and in his unfinished tale *The Notion Club Papers* that he wrote in the early 1940s. But the term seems to indicate a kind of visionary experience, or what Tolkien would call a "waking dream."[16] Tolkien is elusive in the way that he speaks about Faërian Drama and Elvish Enchantment, never quite committing to saying this is something that can occur in the real world. Tolkien presents Faërian Drama as a real experience, but he speaks of Elves and the realm of Faërie in a dual and even contradictory way, sometimes as though Elves are real and Faërie an actual place, other times as though they are merely the invention of the human imagination, existing only in a realm of unreality.[17] In a few different essays and commentaries, the scholar Verlyn Flieger has engaged with Tolkien's most contradictory and paradoxical statements in "On Fairy-Stories," drawing not only on his published text, but on the earlier manuscript drafts of

---

15 Tolkien, *On Fairy-Stories*, 63; Tolkien, "The Notion Club Papers," 193.

16 Tolkien, *The Fellowship of the Ring*, I, iii, 81.

17 Tolkien, *On Fairy-Stories*, 32.

the essay as well. Flieger notes: "Anticipating a skeptical reception, Tolkien tries in the essay as in his letters to have it both ways, on the one hand treating elves as real beings independent of humanity, and on the other hand saying that they are products of human imagination."[18] He is never clear where he stands, expressing the ambiguity of his position in the modern era. In the modernity of Tolkien's time, secular disenchantment and religious tradition stood as pillars of a world view undergoing deep transformation.

Tolkien uses the term "Sub-creation" because, as a devout Catholic, Tolkien saw himself and other artists and authors as creators under God. Such artists are not the instigators of primary Creation, but rather instruments through whom the divine imagination can be channeled and shaped. Tolkien illustrates this idea in a series of lines from his poem *Mythopoeia*:

> Man, Sub-creator, the refracted Light
> through whom is splintered from a single White
> to many hues, and endlessly combined
> in living shapes that move from mind to mind.[19]

---

18 Verlyn Flieger, "But What Did He Really Mean?" *Tolkien Studies* 11 (2014): 155.

19 Tolkien, *On Fairy Stories*, 65.

The human being is able to refract and reshape the divine inspiration into art and creative works, which then continue to refract as others participate in that art. Our reading of *The Lord of the Rings*, and our experience of seeing the images that arise when we engage in the story, are such a creative participation. We are each prisms, shaping the light of God into an iridescent infinity of sub-creations. Yet those sub-creations also contain within them the primal creative white light of God, the source of the primary imagination.

Tolkien said that literature might be the best medium for sub-creation because of its ability to evoke images directly from the imagination of the reader. The written or spoken word can communicate a universal and a particular simultaneously.[20] The word is both concrete and fluid, and leaps from imagination to imagination. As Tolkien eloquently explicates:

> Literature works from mind to mind and is thus more progenitive. It is at once more universal and more poignantly particular. If it speaks of *bread* or *wine* or *stone* or *tree*, it appeals to the whole of these things, to their ideas; yet each hearer will give to them a peculiar personal embodiment in

---

20 Tolkien, *On Fairy-Stories*, 61.

his imagination.... If a story says "he climbed a hill and saw a river in the valley below," the illustrator may catch, or nearly catch, his own vision of such a scene; but every hearer of the words will have his own picture, and it will be made out of all the hills and rivers and dales he has ever seen, but especially out of The Hill, The River, The Valley which were for him the first embodiment of the word.[21]

One can hear the archetypal to which Tolkien is speaking in this passage: The Hill, The River, The Valley are all capitalized in that final sentence. The written word is able to communicate not only the particular images as they arise in the imagination of the author, but it also connects to the universal or the archetype behind that unique image. The image communicated thus has both a quality of being ancient or even eternal, but also of being newly made or perceived in that moment.

---

21 Tolkien, *On Fairy-Stories*, 82, n. E.

Misty Mountains

2

The Fellowship of the Ring – *Book II*
From the Misty Mountains to the Great River

AS BOOK II OPENS we find we have crossed the threshold of the Bruinen, the Loudwater River that marks the border to Rivendell from the surrounding wilds. We enter into a new kind of world, one fully steeped in enchantment and Elvish memory—memories of a lost, ancient world. We find ourselves in Rivendell, in the house of Elrond, with the first chapter, "**Many Meetings.**" And there are many meetings indeed! First, Gandalf fills in Frodo on the missing elements of his story, between when he lost consciousness at the ford and when he awoke in Rivendell four nights and three days later. We learn more of what the Ringwraiths really are, and how Frodo was well on his way to becoming one of their kind. And Gandalf speaks of the Eldar, the High Elves, who dwell in Rivendell, such as Glorfindel who came to Frodo's rescue right before the flight to the ford. Gandalf says that the Eldar—which is one of the many names for the High Elves, one of the kindreds of which is the

Noldor—are those who have at one time lived in the Blessed Realm, or the Undying Lands in the uttermost West beyond the confines of the world. Because they once dwelt in the Blessed Realm, these Elves live at once in both worlds, and have great power against both the Seen and Unseen. This is why Frodo saw Glorfindel as a blazing figure of white light as he crossed into the otherworld himself.

Glorfindel was born in the Blessed Realm and lived for many years in the hidden city of Gondolin during the First Age of the World. He is one of the Elves who was slain and then reborn, sent back to Middle-earth as an emissary from the Valar, the divine Powers of the world. Gandalf calls Glorfindel one of the Firstborn, which is yet another name for those of Elvish race. The Elves are called the Firstborn because the first generation of Elves were the first of the Children of Ilúvatar, or Children of God, to awaken in the newly made world. The Firstborn awoke by the shores of Cuiviénen in the beginning of the First Age, even before the Sun or Moon was made. The Elves awoke beneath the stars, and called themselves the Quendi, or those who speak.

In this scene by Frodo's bedside, Gandalf also reflects to himself on Frodo's condition, noting that there seems to be a hint of transparency to him. He says to himself of Frodo: "He may become like a glass filled with a clear light for eyes to see that can."[1] This remarkable statement brings to mind an image from several chapters later in this same book, when in the chapter "Farewell to Lórien" Galadriel gives Frodo the crystal phial containing water from her mirror, in which is captured the light of Eärendil, the wandering planet that is named Venus in our world. There is an echo between Gandalf's intuition of what Frodo will become, and the gift that Galadriel gives him. They are both a glass filled with clear light, for eyes to see that can.

At the feast in Frodo's honor, we see Elrond for the first time (or the first time since his appearance in *The Hobbit*). Elrond's grey eyes have light in them like the light of stars, and he is mighty among both Elves and Men. He is called the "Half-Elven." The reason is because of Elrond's lineage, for he is a descendent of both mortal and immortal bloodlines. Elrond is the son of Eärendil, who sails his ship Vingilot through the heavens as a wandering planet. This is why Aragorn says to Bilbo that it was "his affair" if he had the "cheek" to make verses about Eärendil in the house of Elrond.[2] If Bilbo was going to dare composing a poem about Elrond's own father in his house, he would need to get all the details right!

1 Tolkien, *The Fellowship of the Ring*, II, i, 217.
2 Tolkien, *The Fellowship of the Ring*, II, i, 231.

Here is opportune moment to look at these important lineages: Elrond is the son of Eärendil, who himself was the son of an elf-woman named Idril Celebrindal and a mortal man named Tuor. Furthermore, Elrond's mother is named Elwing, and she is the granddaughter of the elf-woman Lúthien Tinúviel and the mortal man Beren, whose story I mentioned in Chapter One. Thus, Elrond is half mortal and half elf from both sides. However, there is more to this story of Elvish and mortal lineages. Elrond had a brother, named Elros. Like all Half-elven, they were given a choice of which kindred to which they could belong: Elf or mortal. Elrond chose to be an immortal Elf, and has lived to see Three Ages of the world. But Elros chose to be mortal, and became the first king of the island of Númenor. He was granted long life, a full five hundred years before he died. From him the line of kings descends, all the way through Elendil and Isildur—the king who cut the One Ring from Sauron's hand during the Last Alliance. Thus, the lineage of Aragorn is also made clear: he is the direct descendent of Isildur, the last heir to the kingdoms of Arnor and Gondor founded by the Númenoreans.

At this feast in Frodo's honor we meet another important figure, although we do not see nearly as much of her as one might wish. This is Arwen Undómiel, the daughter of Elrond and Celebrían. It is said of Arwen that in her the likeness of Lúthien Tinúviel (her great great grandmother) came on Earth once again. As we know from Aragorn's tale, Lúthien died a mortal death alongside Beren, and thus Arwen cannot be a reincarnation of Lúthien, as can occur when Elves die. An elf, although immortal, can die in battle or from grief. But they can then be reborn into a new body, for their spirits are bound to the circles of the world as long as the world shall last. Although there are only hints of their relationship throughout the story, Arwen is the great love of Aragorn. Their story is told in full in Appendix A at the end of *The Return of the King*.[3] But I recommend not reading this until after you have finished reading all of *The Lord of the Rings*.

Arwen's lineage also is worth tracing, because not only is Elrond her father, but her mother Celebrian is the daughter of Galadriel and Celeborn, the Lady and Lord of Lothlórien. As we learn in just a single line in the chapter "Many Meetings," Celebrian was tormented by orcs, and although she survived, she chose to depart Middle-earth forever and sail into the West

---

[3] The Appendices contain backstory from the First and Second Ages, as well as a rich timeline of the Third Age, up to and through the narrative of *The Lord of the Rings* itself, and even beyond the end of the story. They also discuss family trees, calendars, and—of greatest significance to Tolkien—writing and languages.

to the Undying Lands. She could not stay in the mortal realms bearing the suffering she had. Thus Arwen and her two brothers, Elladan and Elrohir, remain in Middle-earth with their father, Elrond. The name of one of the brothers, Elladan, holds a key to his family lineage: *adan* means "man," as we also saw in the name "Dúnadan," or "Man of the West" that is given by Glorfindel to Aragorn. And *ell* in this usage means "elf," so the name "Elladan: translates as "elf-man," which is fitting for one of the half-elven. Furthermore, the Elvish word "El," as used in the names Elrond and Elros, translates as "Star." Through both their language and their names, an intimate connection is reflected between the Elves and the stars.

After the feast, the company moves to the Hall of Fire, where songs and tales are shared throughout the night. The Hall of Fire, from my perspective, recalls the creation story of the world itself, the Music of the Ainur. In this cosmogony, the *Ainulindalë*, the Ainur sing the world into form, and Ilúvatar—the One God—grants it being and reality through what is called the Secret Fire. So the world was born through music and fire, and this is recapitulated in the Hall of Fire in Rivendell. Here Frodo experiences what we might call a Faërian Drama, right before Bilbo shares his verses about Eärendil.

We hear of places in the land of Beleriand, the western section of the continent of Middle-earth that sank beneath the sea at the end of the First Age: the coastal region Arvernien, located in the southwest of Beleriand, contained the birchwood forest Nimbrethil, both of which Bilbo mentions in his song. He also speaks of Elwing, Eärendil's wife and mother to Elrond. Bilbo says she is flying, for Elwing had developed the ability to turn herself into a white seabird. When Eärendil is sailing, with the shining jewel of the Silmaril bound to his brow, he sees the Undying Lands: Valinor, the city of the gods, and Eldamar, also called Elvenhome. The many places named in this verse are all in the Blessed Realm: Tirion, which is an Elvish city, and the Shadowmere, a body of water near to it. The Elder King mentioned here is Manwë, who is husband to Elbereth, queen of the stars. They are the two highest Valar, the Powers of the world. They live in the palatial dwelling called Ilmarin, also mentioned in Bilbo's verse, which stands atop the mountain Taniquetil.

Tolkien painted an image of Taniquetil in 1928, and titled it "Halls of Manwë on the Mountains of the World above Faërie."[4] The positioning of the Sun and the Moon

---

4 Wayne G. Hammond and Christina Scull, *J. R. R. Tolkien: Artist & Illustrator* (New York: Houghton Mifflin, 2000), 56.

in this painting is significant, and peculiar. The mountain divides night from day, and we see the daylight Sun on the left and the crescent Moon on the right. But if one looks carefully, the crescent of the Moon is bending *away* from the Sun—something we never see in the primary world where the light of the Moon is caused by the reflected light of the Sun. Here, in the imaginal world of Faërie, the Moon makes its own light and waxes and wanes for its own, enchanted reasons.

This scene in the Hall of Fire ends with an Elvish hymn to Elbereth: *"A Elbereth Gilthoniel, silivren penna miriel."*[5] Below is a direct English translation of the words:

A Elbereth Gilthoniel
O Star-Queen, Star-Kindler

silivren penna miriel
(white) glittering slants down sparkling like jewels

o menel aglar elenath!
From firmament glory (of the) star-host!

Na-chaered palan-díriel
To-remote distance after having gazed

---

5 Tolkien, *The Fellowship of the Ring*, II, i, 231.

o galadhremmin ennorath
from treewoven middle-earth,

Fanuilos le linnathon
Snow-white, to thee I will chant

nef aear, si nef aearon!
on this side of the ocean, here on this side of the great ocean![6]

The translation doesn't have the same poetic rhythm as the original Elvish, which has an AABABCC rhyme scheme. This particular translation comes from Ruth Noel, in her slim but extremely useful book *The Languages of Tolkien's Middle-Earth*, which I highly recommend to anyone interested in the languages of Middle-earth. Learning these languages is the key to understanding the meanings of all the names in Tolkien's stories. Each name contains its own story of the life and lineage of the figure or place that bears it.

The following chapter, "**The Council of Elrond**," is perhaps the most hefty chapter of the entire book, filled with lore and ancient history. Chapter two is another of those "research chapters" that I mentioned

---

6   Noel, *The Languages of Tolkien's Middle-Earth*, 37.

previously. It can be helpful to return to this chapter throughout the story, if you need clarification on the history or further information about names or events.

Elrond makes a telling statement near the beginning of this chapter: the Council must deem what to do with the Ring.

> That is the purpose for which you are called hither. Called, I say, though I have not called you to me, strangers from distant lands. You come and are here met, in this very nick of time, by chance as it may seem. Yet it is not so. Believe rather that it is so ordered that we, who sit here, and none others, must now find counsel for the peril of the world.[7]

This is not the kind of statement one usually hears, at least in the modern world. There is trust in the divine workings that lie behind so-called "chance." Indeed, it is valuable to make note of every time the word "chance," or the phrase "a chance meeting," appears in *The Lord of the Rings*. The Tolkien scholar Tom Shippey has observed whenever Tolkien uses the word "chance" in his stories, he is implying a deeper meaning than the

---

[7] Tolkien, *The Fellowship of the Ring*, II, ii, 236.

word "chance" would necessarily entail.[8] It points to something beyond mere chance or coincidence, but rather to a synchronicity, or a divine patterning or intention. "Just chance brought me then, if chance you will call it," Tom Bombadil remarks, when he encounters the hobbits in the Old Forest entrapped by Old Man Willow.[9] Gandalf comments that the White Council drove Sauron out from his stronghold in Mirkwood "in the very year of the finding of this Ring: a strange chance, if chance it was."[10] Bilbo puts his hand on the Ring in the dark tunnel beneath the Misty Mountains by seeming chance. Yet Gandalf remarks on this incident to Frodo:

> Behind that there was something else at work, beyond any design of the Ring-maker. I can put it no plainer than by saying that Bilbo was *meant* to find the Ring, and *not* by its maker. In which case you also were *meant* to have it. And that may be an encouraging thought.[11]

---

8 Tom Shippey, *The Road to Middle-Earth: How J. R. R. Tolkien Created a New Mythology* (New York: Houghton Mifflin, 2003), 152.
9 Tolkien, *The Fellowship of the Ring*, I, vii, 123.
10 Tolkien, *The Fellowship of the Ring*, II, ii, 244.
11 Tolkien, *The Fellowship of the Ring*, I, vii, 54–55.

Other such examples abound throughout Tolkien's legendarium, some more or less ambiguous in their meaning. "A chance-meeting, as we say in Middle-earth."[12] Elrond did not call this Council, it was orchestrated by chance—or perhaps, by the divine.

We learn in this Council of the long history of the Ring, and of the Elven-smiths of Eregion, and the master craftsman Celebrimbor. Celebrimbor is the grandson of Fëanor, who made the three great Silmarils that are the primary subject of *The Silmarillion*. Renowned craftsmanship runs in that lineage. Here too we hear once more of Númenor and the Last Alliance. Even though these ancient stories are told in brief, they are mentioned repeatedly throughout *The Lord of the Rings*, so we begin to get a sense of the most important events in the long history of Middle-earth. If you ever feel confusion about the references being made in this chapter, I recommend checking the map. It can help orient you in space, so you can see the locations where these events unfolded. You can see where the lost kingdom of Arnor is in the north, and the long-standing kingdom of Gondor in the south, near the mouths of the Great River, Anduin.

---

12 Tolkien, *Unfinished Tales: Of Númenor and Middle-Earth*, ed. Christopher Tolkien, (New York: Houghton Mifflin, 1980), 326.

When Elrond recalls the Last Alliance, he reminisces over the hosts of Beleriand, the land that was the western region of the continent of Middle-earth, which sank at the end of the First Age. When Elrond speaks of the breaking of Thangorodrim, he is describing the ancient realm of the original Dark Lord, Morgoth. Mordor is but an echo and an imitation of Thangorodrim, just as Sauron was but a servant of Morgoth.

Elrond also briefly recounts how Isildur took the Ring for himself, and how he perished in the Gladden Fields by the Great River. Only the shards of the sword Narsil were brought out of that ruin, by Ohtar, the squire of Isildur who happened to survive the ambush by orcs. Elrond says that since the Last Alliance the race of Númenor has decayed and the span of their years has lessened. He is speaking about his own brother, Elros, and his lineage. Elros lived for five hundred years, but with each generation after Elendil and Isildur, the lifespan of the Númenoreans has shortened. So as the final descendent of that line, how old is Aragorn? At this moment in *The Lord of the Rings*, he is eighty-seven years old, and will turn eighty-eight on March 1 of the following year. This is the prime of life for one of Númenorean descent, with their comingled Elvish and human blood.

We also learn of the chief cities in Gondor, the kingdom to the south. There were once three cities there:

Minas Ithil, the Tower of the Rising Moon, built to the east on the very slopes of the Mountains of Shadow bordering Mordor; Minas Anor, the Tower of the Setting Sun, built to the west on the slopes of the White Mountains; and between them was the chief city, Osgiliath, whose name means the Citadel of Stars. So we have the Sun, Moon, and stars all represented by the Gondorian citadels. *Ithil* means "Moon" in Elvish, *Anor* means "Sun." These were some of the first Elvish words that came to Tolkien, recorded at least as early as 1915. *Giliath* means "host of stars," with *gil* meaning "star," and the suffix *ath* making them plural, as in a host of stars.

The names of the Towers of the Sun and Moon change over the course of history. Eventually, Sauron's Ringwraiths conquer Minas Ithil, and it is renamed Minas Morgul, the Tower of Sorcery. And thus Minas Anor becomes the Tower of Guard, or Minas Tirith as we know it in the Third Age. Again, it can be helpful to look at the map to locate all these places in Gondor, even at this earlier stage in the story. The men of Gondor defend the Great River from the Argonath to the Sea. The Argonath we see near the end of *The Fellowship of the Ring*, when the company travel by boat down the Great River and pass the two magnanimous stone statues of the kingly brothers Isildur and Anárion, the sons of Elendil.

After Elrond speaks, we hear from Boromir of how Gondor fares in the south. He mentions that the only allies who come to Gondor's aid are the men of Rohan—a place and people that will become important in *The Two Towers*. Part of what can be difficult about reading this chapter is the sheer number of names that are mentioned. These references always make more sense upon a later reading. The names may not stick the first time, but when you read them again later, your memory recalls something you have heard before, even if you cannot locate it. This is part of what makes the world of Middle-earth have such depth and richness: the repetition of names and places, without overt explanation of who or what they are. We learn the history of Middle-earth through immersion in its languages and cultures.

Boromir was sent on his quest not because of any external occurrence but because of a dream: a dream that his brother Faramir had repeatedly, and that he himself had once. The dream is a prophecy, and once again we see the importance of dream, vision, and foresight elevated in this tale, and the world view that Tolkien expresses through it.

During the Council, we hear stated in full who Aragorn truly is, and the noble lineage of which he is a descendent. There have been hints throughout regarding his heritage, but here we finally learn that he is the direct descendent of Isildur and heir to the thrones of both Arnor and Gondor. Recall the vision the hobbits had upon the Barrow-downs, when Tom Bombadil was speaking of the sons of forgotten kings who go wandering in the wilderness, guarding against evil things. The hobbits have a vision of lineage of Men, each bearing a sword, and the last has a star upon his brow. This vision that the four hobbits collectively experienced is of Aragorn—who they "chanced" to meet later that very day in Bree—and of Aragorn's lineage of the Men of Westernesse, or Númenor. Those men of Westernesse have dwindled and become simply the Rangers of the North, who guard against the servants of the Enemy. They are the sons of forgotten kings.

To complete the long history of the Ring, Gandalf tells his own tale, the final story of the Council. He speaks of how he went to Gondor to read Isildur's account of his finding of the Ring, and that he was given reluctant admittance to those records by Denethor, the steward of Gondor and the father of Boromir. Here is where he learns the final test, the test of putting the Ring into the heat of a fire—which he conducted right in Frodo's sitting room in Bag-End—that showed him the ring was indeed Sauron's One Ring.

Here too we learn of the betrayal of Saruman, the great wizard who was head of the White Council. Many often find it confusing that Sauron and Saruman have such similar names. For Tolkien, they would not have sounded similar at all, because the meanings behind their names differ so greatly: Sauron means "the abhorred" or "detestable," while Saruman is a Westron translation of the name Curunir, which means "man of skill" in Sindarin Elvish.

Gandalf's and Saruman's conversations in this narrative carry deep wisdom and insight, and one line that stands out in particular is when Saruman speaks of the color white as a beginning, a page to be overwritten, or a light to be broken into many hues. Gandalf says: "In which case it is no longer white.... And he that breaks a thing to find out what it is has left the path of wisdom."[13] Indeed, Saruman has left the path of wisdom in his arrogance and desire for power. Tolkien's words echo those of William Wordsworth, who declared: "We murder to dissect."[14] One is reminded of the reductionism that has defined so much of modern rationalism, and shaped the scientific world view that led to the rampant industrialization of the twentieth century. Tolkien was keenly aware of the negative consequences of industrialization, seeing his beloved, rural childhood home of

---

13 Tolkien, *The Fellowship of the Ring*, II, ii, 252.
14 William Wordsworth, "The Tables Turned."

Sarehole sacrificed on behalf of so-called progress and economic efficiency.

When we hear of Gandalf's imprisonment on the rooftop of Orthanc, and of his rescue by the eagle Gwaihir, Frodo explains that he saw Gandalf there in a dream—the first dream Frodo had in the house of Tom Bombadil and Goldberry. Again, foresight is present here—or in this case Frodo is seeing events taking place elsewhere in Middle-earth through his dream vision.

When Gandalf has at last finished his tale, we come to the most pivotal moment in the story: what to do with the Ring. The options are debated and weighed, and discarded one by one. Gandalf makes the important point: "It is not our part here to take thought only for a season, or for a few lives of Men, or for a passing age of the world. We should seek a final end of this menace, even if we do not hope to make one."[15] This is an extraordinary statement: they must take thought for the well-being of the world as it endures throughout time. Can you imagine if we made decisions with such forethought in our world today? What a resilient, and potentially more harmonious, world in which we might live.

They conclude that the Ring must be destroyed in the fire in which it was made, Orodruin, or as it is called

---

15 Tolkien, *The Fellowship of the Ring*, II, ii, 260.

in the common tongue, Mount Doom. One might ask why someone such as Tolkien, who knew so much about language and created so many diverse words, would call this essential place Mount Doom. But the word "doom" itself has a storied linguistic lineage, coming from Old English by way of Germany. The Old English word "doom" means "judgment," and shares the Proto-Germanic root for "to do" and "to put in place." Doom is related to fate, destiny, and final judgment.

There seems to be some doom, or fate at work when Frodo volunteers to carry the Ring into Mordor. He feels as though some other will is using his voice as he speaks. When Elrond says, "This task is appointed to you, Frodo; and if you do not find a way, no one will," he is not saying it was appointed by anyone at the Council.[16] It was appointed in the same way that the Council itself was called together: by chance. Frodo's fate is divinely chosen—and yet, paradoxically, he steps into it of his own free will. Fate and free will intermingle here, in the most profound of ways.

I have dwelled at some length on this chapter because of its great importance to the unfolding of the rest of the story. From here forward, the tale unfolds far more swiftly, moving from one dynamic landscape

---

16 Tolkien, *The Fellowship of the Ring*, II, ii, 264.

to the next. We see so much of Middle-earth in the following eight chapters.

Before the Fellowship sets off in the third chapter, **"The Ring Goes South,"** news is brought to Rivendell from every corner of the land. The secret errand to a strange country down the Silverlode carried out by the sons of Elrond is actually a mission to Galadriel in Lothlórien, as we can piece together from what we later learn about that land. So here we understand that she already knew of the Fellowship's coming, and was prepared to welcome the company.

Nine companions are chosen intentionally, representing the Free Peoples of Middle-earth. A wealth of symbolism adheres to the members of the company, and what they each can represent. We can perceive different bonds between them all that shift and change over the course of the story: Frodo, Sam, and Aragorn; Merry, Pippin, and Boromir; Legolas and Gimli; Gandalf. The counsels taken between Gandalf and Aragorn. The connection between Aragorn and Frodo. Gandalf as guide, Frodo as innocent hero. The animosity and subsequent friendship of the Dwarf and Elf. The tension between the two Men. The older and younger pairings of the four hobbits. Just as we see in the verses about the Great Rings that open the book, the symbolism of numbers is significant to Tolkien.

Before departing Rivendell, the shards of the sword Narsil are reforged into Andúril, the Flame of the West, and it is inscribed with the symbols of Aragorn's lineage: the crescent Moon and rayed Sun, and the seven stars of Númenor. These are the same celestial symbols represented by the three ancient cities of Gondor, Minas Ithil, Minas Anor, and Osgiliath.

The day on which the company of the Ring depart is said to be near the end of December. If we look in Appendix B, "The Tale of Years," we can see that the Fellowship leaves on December 25, a significant date in the Christian calendar, and therefore a date of numinous meaning to Tolkien himself.

Time moves much more quickly and with less detail in this chapter, until the company reaches Hollin, or the deserted Elvish land called Eregion where Celebrimbor and the other Elven ring-smiths dwelt long ago. Here too we learn the seemingly innumerable names of the three great peaks in the middle of the range of the Misty Mountains, names in Elvish, Dwarvish, and English. The failed attempt to cross the pass of Caradhras shows us the agency of the land itself—it is the mountain that hinders the company's passage, through its own will against them. We can see how the landscapes and regions of Middle-earth are themselves alive and seemingly conscious. The company debates whether this is the power of the enemy, but it seems to me this is the mountain itself barring the Fellowship from crossing.

So they turn to a different path, the road that Gandalf had suggested as an alternative to Aragorn's desire to cross Caradhras. In chapter four, "A Journey in the Dark," the Fellowship passes into the realm of Moria. Many mysteries surround Moria. Why is there a lake at its western gate? What kind of creature is the Watcher in the Water, and how did it get there? Why does it immediately seize Frodo, the bearer of the Ring? Moria Gate itself is an impressive piece of artwork, one of few works co-created in harmony by Elves and Dwarves together. The Doors of Durin were made during the same era in which the Great Rings were forged. Before Gandalf figures out the riddle to the doorway, he commands them to open in Elvish: *Annon edhellen*, doors of the Elves, *edro hi ammen*, open now for us, *Fennas nogothrim*, gates of the Dwarves, *lasto beth lammen*, listen to the word of my voice.[17]

When the Fellowship finally enters the mines, the long, dark journey commences. Even though it seems they might often be lost, Aragorn assures that company that they could not have a better guide than Gandalf.

---

[17] Tolkien, *The Fellowship of the Ring*, II, iv, 299; Noel, *The Languages of Tolkien's Middle-Earth*, 38.

He says: "He is surer of finding the way home in a blind night than the cats of Queen Berúthiel."[18] This is one of the very few statements in all of the legendarium of Middle-earth on which Tolkien could not elaborate further. He simply did not know more about the cats of Queen Berúthiel—and yet, he had to include this mysterious statement from Aragorn.[19]

We are given but a glimpse of the fallen majesty of the Dwarvish kingdom of Dwarrowdelf, of Khazad-dûm. The word "dwarrow" is actually the ancient plural word for dwarf.[20] And the more common plural "dwarves" is a neologism of Tolkien's, who felt "dwarves" and "elves" sounded far better than the apparently correct "dwarfs" and "elfs." Gimli's song of Khazad-dûm refers to the history of the First Age, when he mentions Gondolin and Nargothrond, two mighty Elvish kingdoms of old.

When the company arrives at Balin's tomb, Tolkien himself halted in writing the tale. He was stuck, and he did not know how to proceed. After a long delay, he went back to the beginning and rewrote much of what he had set down. This was Tolkien's way. He would

---

18 Tolkien, *The Fellowship of the Ring*, II, iv, 303.
19 Tolkien, *Letters*, 228.
20 Tolkien, *Letters*, 23.

rewrite and then move forward, rewrite again and then once more move forward. He was polishing the rough gems that he had found in the imaginal realm into a story that others could also enter.

The fifth chapter, "**The Bridge of Khazad-dûm**," shows the first major violent conflict in which the Fellowship is engaged—besides the brief skirmish in Eregion with the wargs. This is the first encounter with orcs, and the first time all of the members of the Fellowship are engaged in battle. Frodo is almost lost here, protected only by his *mithril* coat. The word *mithril* translates as "grey brilliance," and shares a root with the name "Mithrandir" by which Gandalf the Grey is at times called.

Grey is a significant color for Tolkien, appearing not only as the eye color of many important characters, but also in names such as the Grey Havens and the Grey Elves. In a story seemingly built on the contrast between dark and light, the color grey indicate liminality and ambiguity. The Grey Elves, or the Sindar, are those who, as told in *The Silmarillion*, began the journey toward the divine light of the Blessed Realm but instead turned aside, choosing to stay in Middle-earth. The Sindar become sundered in language and culture from their kindred who travel into the Undying West to witness the sacred light. They are a people in between, drawn toward the light and yet in love with the shadows of the mortal lands. Likewise, the Grey Havens are a harbor on the westernmost shores of Middle-earth, the departure point for the Elves who choose to leave Middle-earth for Tol Eressëa, the immortal Elvenhome. The Grey Havens also stand as a threshold between realms.

Upon the bridge itself Gandalf faces the Balrog, a demon of the First Age of the world. A Balrog is a Maia, the same kind of spirit that Gandalf is, and that Sauron is also. They are matched in power, although Gandalf is incarnated in a comparatively frail human form at this time. The Balrog appears as a "dark figure streaming with fire," a terror made of shadow and flame.[21] Gandalf calls the Balrog "flame of Udûn," which was one of the many names of the original Dark Lord Morgoth's first lair to the north of Beleriand.[22] The Balrog serves a master older and more evil even than Sauron. Gandalf identifies himself as a servant of the Secret Fire. The Secret Fire is that which dwells with Ilúvatar, the One God. The Secret Fire gives life and being to all. Gandalf is a servant of the One God who dwells beyond the world. He also says he is a wielder of the flame of Anor, which refers to the Sun. The Sun was

---

21 Tolkien, *The Fellowship of the Ring*, II, v, 322.
22 Tolkien, *The Fellowship of the Ring*, II, v, 322.

sent into the sky in part to bring fear into the hearts of the servants of Morgoth. The Sun, who is female in this mythology, casts light onto the shadows spread by the Dark Lord. The servants of the enemy fear the light of the Sun, and many cannot travel beneath her brilliant rays.

The bridge breaks, and Gandalf is pulled into the abyss. His loss is irreparable. It feels impossible that Gandalf, of all the members of the Fellowship, could be the one to die. We meet true grief here, a tragedy beyond belief.

The following three chapters, **"Lothlórien,"** "The Mirror of Galadriel," and "Farewell to Lórien," all take place within the Golden Wood, the realm of the Lady Galadriel. Lothlórien is the closest we come to seeing what Faërie really looks like in Middle-earth. As Frodo reflects to himself: "In Rivendell there was memory of ancient things; in Lórien the ancient things still lived on in the waking world."[23] The timelessness of Faërie is preserved in Lórien, as we come to learn in the following chapter, "The Mirror of Galadriel." The quality of timelessness is preserved through Galadriel's wielding of Nenya, one of the Three Rings of the Elves, which is hidden in her keeping.

---

23 Tolkien, *The Fellowship of the Ring*, II, vi, 340.

The entire company crosses into Lórien with their eyes blinded, and this too is significant. In tales about crossing into Faërie, the senses are often obscured. In *Smith of Wootton Major*, the one tale Tolkien composed explicitly about Faërie, he describes the protagonist's experience of passing between the lands surrounding the village in which he lives, and the Land of Faërie that shares its borders: "He was guided and guarded, but he had little memory of the ways he had taken; for often he had been blindfolded by mist or by shadow, until at last he came to a high place under a night-sky of innumerable stars."[24] Only after the threshold has been crossed does clear sight return—and that sight is often clearer and more poignant than it had been in the physical world of the senses. With his eyesight obscured, Frodo's other senses are piqued, taking in sounds and scents of the changing world. When at last their blindfolds are removed, Frodo sees the world as though it was both ancient and newly made. This is what it is like to glimpse the archetypal—it is both eternal and ever-new. As Sam also looks about the glade in Lothlórien, he says to Frodo: "I feel as if I was *inside* a song, if

---

24 Tolkien, *Smith of Wootton Major*, ed. Verlyn Flieger, (London: HarperCollins, 2005), 31.

you take my meaning."[25] A linguist would indeed take the meaning of what he says, and the meaning of the thought behind it. To be inside a song is to be en-chanted. This is the magic of Faërie, the spell one enters upon crossing its threshold.

In this place of Cerin Amroth, we see Aragorn wrapped in a waking memory, as though he has stepped back through time. He says *"Arwen vanimelda, namarië!"*[26] Arwen, fair-love, farewell.[27] This was the place that many years before Arwen and Aragorn pled their troth, swore their love for each other. And here Aragorn says farewell to her and that memory, not knowing whether he will survive the perils before him, and bring their love to fruition.

In the seventh chapter, **"The Mirror of Galadriel,"** we meet Galadriel and Celeborn. Galadriel was born in the Blessed Realm, and is of the Golden House of Finarfin, one of the great houses of the Noldorin who lived in the West and then went into exile in Middle-earth after the Silmarils were stolen by Morgoth. Galadriel is a fascinating figure, a rebel and an athlete in her earlier years, and now a queen of wisdom, grace, and virtuous

25 Tolkien, *The Fellowship of the Ring*, II, vi, 342.
26 Tolkien, *The Fellowship of the Ring*, II, vi, 343.
27 Noel, *The Languages of Tolkien's Middle-Earth*, 38.

power. Galadriel and Celeborn settled in Lothlórien during the First Age, even before the great kingdoms of Gondolin and Nargothrond fell in Beleriand. They have had a relationship with this land for millennia. When Sam and Frodo are discussing the Elves, Sam remarks that their magic seems to be down deep, a part of the land itself. The Elves and the Golden Wood have been shaping each other, their subtle magic working reciprocally in interrelationship.

There is little I wish to say yet about the visions Sam and then Frodo behold in the Mirror of Galadriel. We do not yet know what we are seeing, and where in the timeline of the story they land. Are they the future, the present, the deep past? I will return to the Mirror throughout the remainder of this journey, as the visions become relevant. There is one vision though upon which I want to comment, when Frodo sees the Sea rising in a great storm, and the red Sun sinking in the clouds, and the tall ship sailing up out of the West. These are visions of the drowning of Númenor. He sees a river flowing through a populous city: this is Osgiliath, in Gondor. The white fortress with seven towers is the city of Minas Tirith. The banner with the emblem of the white tree is the symbol of the House of Elendil.

The last vision Frodo sees is of Sauron's Eye, and this is one of the only glimpses we receive of the Dark

Lord. The second glimpse is when Frodo is seated upon Amon Hen in the final chapter of Book II, "The Breaking of the Fellowship." In both visions Frodo beholds Sauron's terrible Eye, the single eye of outward-gazing vision. This single eye does not self-reflect, but looks only out into the world. It cannot see its own Shadow, and thus becomes subsumed by that Shadow, so that is all the world can see.

We witness hereafter Galadriel's test of her character, as she is freely offered the Ring, sees what she could become, and is able to resist that. By succeeding in that test she also surrenders to the realization that she will fade and diminish, as all Elves in Middle-earth are fated to do. She must pass over into the West at last, so that she may remain herself and not be consumed by the desire for power.

In the eighth chapter, **"Farewell to Lórien,"** Galadriel's first song recalls many of the locations in the Uttermost West of which Bilbo also sang in his verses about Eärendil: Eldamar, Tirion, Ilmarin. She is longing to return there, after her many thousands of years in exile.

The gift-giving then begins, and this feels like a sacred event. Galadriel gives Aragorn a sheathe for Andúril, and then asks if there is anything else he desires. He responds by saying: "Lady, you know all my desire, and long held in keeping the only treasure I seek. Yet it is not yours to give me, even if you would; and only through darkness shall I come to it."[28] He is speaking of his love, of Arwen Undómiel, who is the granddaughter of Galadriel. She gives him then the green stone by which he comes by his kingly name, Elessar. In the first chapter of this book, Bilbo said Aragorn advised him to include a green stone in his song about Eärendil. Aragorn felt it was important, and now we can understand why.

The gift Gimli asks for is provocative: a single hair from Galadriel's head. She gives him three, which is beyond what he ever could have hoped. But there is a backstory to this decision: it was said that the golden and silver light of one of the Two Trees of Valinor shone too in Galadriel's hair. The great Elven-smith Fëanor, who forged the Silmarils in which is contained this blended light, three times requested of Galadriel a strand of hair from her head. But she refused him, and thus strife and distrust broke out between them. So in giving the three hairs to Gimli, who so humbly states what he wishes, Galadriel offers him what she refused to Fëanor in ages past. She closes the loop of that story-line, and thereby forges a peace between Elves and Dwarves that had been long broken.

---

28 Tolkien, *The Fellowship of the Ring*, II, viii, 365.

Thus the company leaves Lothlórien, and it seems to slip backward in time—for it is a timeless place—and the Fellowship has reentered the world of linear time once more. In the ninth chapter, **"The Great River,"** we see and learn of many more lands of Middle-earth, and it can once more be helpful to track the progress of the Fellowship on the map. At this stage in the journey Gollum is at last identified as the long-suspected snuffling shadow with luminous eyes that has been tracking the company since Moria.

We come at last to the Argonath, the two great statues of Isildur and Anárion that stand guard over the northern border of Gondor. Here Aragorn is able to witness the likenesses of his forefathers, and for a moment Frodo and Sam are able to see the kingly lineage revealed within him as well, shining through the outer guise of the rugged Ranger.

The final chapter, **"The Breaking of the Fellowship,"** brings hard choices to the company: to go to Minas Tirith, or to cross the river and make the eastern passage to Mordor. The decision is made by Frodo, when he sees how Boromir has succumbed to the temptation of the Ring, and he fears that each member of the company might eventually fall in such a way. When he escapes from Boromir's grasp by putting on the Ring, Frodo sits upon the Seat of Seeing on Amon Hen and is able to gain a broad view of all that is taking place in Middle-earth in that moment. He is then caught between the power of the Eye and a mysterious Voice. The Voice tells him to take it off. "Fool, take it off!"[29] Who is this Voice? It is not Frodo, and certainly not Sauron, but some other power whose identity we will later discover. Frodo finds his will at last, and is able to regain his own agency—and chooses to remove the Ring from his finger. His decision to leave the company is made in that brief, enduring moment.

When the company scatters at Boromir's news of Frodo's sudden disappearance, it is only Sam who keeps his head and works out in his careful way what Frodo would choose to do in that moment. He understands Frodo better than anyone, and can think like him when need be. Again, I must ask is this really the work of a half-wit, as the name Samwise suggests?

So Frodo and Sam set off together, as it should be: not a single hero acting alone, but two humble hobbits, working together in relationship. With their departure, Book II of *The Fellowship of the Ring* comes to a close.

---

29 Tolkien, *The Fellowship of the Ring*, II, x, 392.

Interlude

The Book of Ishness and the Great War

J.R.R. TOLKIEN'S BIOGRAPHER Humphrey Carpenter has described Tolkien as "a man of extreme contrasts. When in a black mood he would feel that there was no hope, either for himself or the world."[1] Yet Tolkien could be lifted out of such a mood by the appearance of a friend or some other shift in scene, and soon find himself in a joyful humor. The roots of that pessimism likely began with the death of his mother, when the young Ronald Tolkien was only twelve years old. But Tolkien experienced many losses in his life.

When Tolkien was sixteen years old he met Edith Bratt, the woman who would eventually become his wife and the mother of their four children. They met while both living in the same boarding house, and she too was an orphan—her mother had died young and her father had disowned her as illegitimate. The young Tolkien was absolutely mesmerized with Edith. However, Tolkien's guardian, the Catholic priest Father Francis

---

1 Carpenter, *Tolkien: A Biography*, 133–34.

Morgan, felt that the beautiful Edith would be a distraction for Tolkien from his studies, and Tolkien needed to focus in order to earn a scholarship at Oxford, where his intellectual abilities would be able to flourish. Without such a scholarship, further education would be inaccessible to Tolkien. So Father Francis Morgan denied the budding romance, and forced Tolkien and Edith apart, forbidding them to meet or even communicate. They endured this enforced separation for three years, from 1910 until Tolkien's twenty-first birthday in 1913.[2] This was an especially dark and reflective period for Tolkien. He also suffered the unexpected death of a close friend during this time: Vincent Trout, who was one of the early members of his schoolboy fellowship the TCBS, or the Tea Club Barrovian Society.[3]

During this period, beginning in December of 1911, J.R.R. Tolkien began making an unusual series of sketches that he came to call *Ishnesses*. The word *Ishness* refers to the symbolic and imaginal quality of these drawings.[4] The drawings contain no explanation, just a title that may or may not correspond clearly with the content of the drawings. The drawings vary widely in

---

2 Carpenter, *Tolkien: A Biography*, 50–51.
3 Garth, *Tolkien and the Great War*, 28.
4 Hammond and Scull, *Artist & Illustrator*, 40.

style and content, but they share in common a raw emotionality evoked by their bold colors, strange shapes, and obscure yet weighty titles. Tolkien made about twenty such visionary drawings between December 1911 and the summer of 1913—with titles such as *Silent, Enormous & Immense, Before, Afterwards, Firelight Magic, Sleep, Undertenishness, Grownupishness, Thought, End of the World*, and *The Back of Beyond*.[5] Many of the images depict an entrance, a crossing of a threshold, or some fantastical landscape. Eventually Tolkien decided these drawings needed a designated notebook of their own. Early in January 1914, Tolkien inscribed in red ink the title *The Book of Ishness* on the beige cloth-covered boards of a Winsor & Newton sketchbook.[6] The book would be the repository for his symbolic and fantastical drawings until 1928, although the greatest outpouring of images came during the years leading up to his enlistment with Kitchener's Army in the Great War.[7]

5   Hammond and Scull, *Artist & Illustrator*, 40.
6   Christina Scull and Wayne G. Hammond, *Reader's Guide, Vol. 2 of The J.R.R. Tolkien Companion and Guide* (New York: Houghton Mifflin, 2006), 40.
7   Hammond and Scull, Artist & Illustrator, 50. Not all of Tolkien's artwork, including a number of drawings from The Book of Ishness, have been published. These images are held safely in the Tolkien Archive at the Bodleian Library in Oxford, where I was lucky enough to be able to view them in 2015. Many of his drawings

One of the earliest of the *Ishnesses*, drawn in 1912, is titled simply *Before*.[8] The illustration depicts a dark corridor lit with flaming torches, leading to a gaping, megalithic doorway from which a red glow issues ominously. The dark, oppressive entryway pulls one's gaze toward the mysterious red glow at the end of the passage. The particular shape of this imposing doorway appears again and again in Tolkien's later writings and artwork, usually accompanied by descriptions of foreboding, fear, and the unknown. It is a doorway underground, a doorway to the underworld.

The drawing *Before* is paired with a following drawing, titled appropriately *Afterwards*, which depicts a solitary figure walking out of a doorway of the same shape as in the previous drawing, and heading down a long hall lit with many torches.[9] *Afterwards* is sketched in yellows and blues. The coloring greatly contrasts the

---

    illustrate the sense that Tolkien's visionary images depict the crossing of a threshold, and a new form of engagement with the imagination. Many drawings from *The Book of Ishness* have been published in Wayne Hammond and Christina Scull's beautiful book *J. R. R. Tolkien: Artist & Illustrator*. Several more of these drawings were more recently made available in the publication *Tolkien: Maker of Middle-Earth*, edited by Catherine McIlwaine to accompany the 2018 exhibition of Tolkien's artwork at the Bodleian Library in Oxford.

8 Hammond and Scull, *Artist & Illustrator*, 34.

9 Hammond and Scull, *Artist & Illustrator*, 36.

stark red and black of *Before*, but also conveys a sense of darkness and gloom. Yet it is less foreboding than the previous drawing. Together, the two images appear to symbolize crossing a threshold, entering an underworld imaginal realm.

Another illustration that portrays the crossing of a threshold is an arresting piece titled *End of the World*. In this drawing a small figure is stepping off a cliff extending over the sea.[10] The Sun shines brightly down onto the scene, and seemingly within the water itself shine white stars, and a crescent Moon bends across the horizon. Yes, the image of a man stepping off a cliff, and the title *End of the World*, seem somber, even depressing. But they convey a dual meaning: this is not only the "end of the world," referring to its demise, or the death of this man, but it is the "end of the world" as in, it is the end of the *known* world. This man has reached the edge and wants to continue his journey. One could see *End of the World* as a symbol of the threshold Tolkien crossed at this time—the doorway to the imaginal, into what he called the realm of Faërie.[11]

---

10 Hammond and Scull, *Artist & Illustrator*, 40.
11 Lance S. Owens, "Lecture I: The Discovery of Faërie," in "J.R.R. Tolkien: An Imaginative Life" (Lecture series presented at Westminster College, Salt Lake City, UT, March 2009), 22:35.

On the verso of this picture another *Ishness* titled *The Back of Beyond*, showing a man lying on his stomach peering over the edge of an open, shuttered doorway or wide window.[12] Behind him stretches a far landscape, with a path leading from the window up into the mountains. Is the figure peering into another realm, an otherworld of the imagination? We can only speculate at the intended meaning of the *Ishnesses* and what Tolkien meant to convey through these evocative, mysterious drawings.

The sense of place—of locality—in the *Ishnesses* is remarkable: not only do many of them seem to convey a symbolic threshold being crossed, but most are oriented within some fantastic landscape. A drawing from January 1914 is titled *Beyond* (which echoes *The Back of Beyond*), and shows in vibrant colors a road leading from a pair of mushroom-shaped trees across a river and into an entryway in the distant indigo mountains.[13] Paired with the drawing are the words: "Alas! in dreadful mood."[14] Likely made at the same time are two other miniscule drawings on a single sheet, one titled *There*

---

12 Catherine McIlwaine, *Tolkien: Maker of Middle-Earth* (Oxford: Bodleian Library, 2018), 41.

13 Hammond and Scull, *Artist & Illustrator*, 42.

14 Tolkien, as quoted in Hammond and Scull, *Artist & Illustrator*, 44.

Interlude: The Book of Ishness *and the Great War* 71

and the other *Here*: the former depicts a triangle around two trees and a mountain, with the words "There (when you don't want to go from here)"; the latter, labeled "Here (in an exciting place)," shows a small circle around three stylized trees or mushrooms, rings like smoke circling the central tree.[15] A few months later, in April 1914, Tolkien made a sketch in this same style named *Everywhere*, showing a range of mountains with a high peak at their center surrounded by a semicircular border.[16] So we have *There*, *Here*, and *Everywhere*.

Everywhere seems to me as though it could be an early prefiguration of a more sophisticated drawing from May 1915, called *The Shores of Faery*.[17] Tolkien wrote a poem just a few months later with the same name in which many of the landscape features of Valinor, the Blessed Realm, are first described. This drawing, *The Shores of Faery*, is also enclosed in a semicircular border, but this border is formed by the Two Trees of Valinor: Silpion (later named Telperion) and Laurelin. The Two Trees of Valinor each give off their own light. The elder tree, Telperion, emanates a silver light, and the younger

---

15 McIlwaine, *Tolkien: Maker of Middle-Earth*, 171.

16 Christina Scull and Wayne G. Hammond, *Chronology*, Vol. 1 of *The J. R. R. Tolkien Companion and Guide* (New York: Houghton Mifflin, 2006), 51.

17 Hammond and Scull, *Artist & Illustrator*, 48.

tree, Laurelin, emanates a golden light. The Two Trees wax and wane for seven hours each, one bright while the other is dim. Twice each day their lights comingle, creating an exquisite twilight of intermingled silver-gold light. When I imagine this light, I envision the kind of strange light one sees during a solar eclipse: neither night nor day, a light not seemingly of this world. That is the light of Faërie.

The Two Trees have their own sad story, which I will not share yet in full, but they met a tragic demise during the First Age of the World. Yet as they perished, one final flower was coaxed forth from Telperion, and one last fruit ripened on the boughs of Laurelin. This last flower became the Moon and the final fruit became the Sun. Many world mythologies have a World Tree or a Tree of Life, but I find it telling that Tolkien's mythology has two. Right at the heart of his legendarium lies this symbol of relationality that plays out in every subsequent story. These are all stories of fellowship, stories of friendship and relationship. The Two Trees of Valinor symbolize that relationality. It is remarkable that Tolkien conceived of the Two Trees of Valinor already in 1915, in this drawing *The Shores of Faery* that he sketched in *The Book of Ishness*. The descendent of the silver tree Telperion can even be heard mentioned in *The Lord of the Rings*: it is the White Tree of Gondor, which descended from Nimloth of Númenor, which descended directly from the Blessed Realm. Everything in Middle-earth has a lineage—even the trees.

So many of the core images in the mythology of Middle-earth came to Tolkien in those early years, leading up to and through the First World War. The War itself had a major effect on Tolkien's psyche, and on the stories that came through his imagination during and after it. By the time the war started, Tolkien's group of friends, the TCBS, had consolidated into a group of four intimate friends: Christopher Wiseman, Rob Gilson, Geoffrey Bache Smith, and John Ronald Tolkien. In the autumn of 1914, Tolkien received a letter from Christopher Wiseman, requesting that they convene with Rob Gilson and G.B. Smith for a "crisis summit": a meeting where they would be free to explore together their most fundamental convictions.[18] These four young men—Wiseman, Gilson, Smith, and Tolkien—formed the "immortal four," as Smith with tragic youthfulness once called the friends.[19] They called the meeting the Council of London, and it was held at Wiseman's home on December 12, 1914.[20] With utmost seriousness and conviction, the

---

18 Garth, *Tolkien and the Great War*, 56.
19 G.B. Smith, as quoted in Carpenter, *Tolkien: A Biography*, 94.
20 Garth, *Tolkien and the Great War*, 57–58.

four friends ranged through a wide agenda, discussing everything from nationalism and patriotic duty, to religion and the complexities of human love, as well as what they saw as their moral obligation to restore goodness and beauty to the world.

Tolkien later reflected that the Council had given him the opportunity of "finding a voice for all kinds of pent up things and a tremendous opening up of everything."[21] Something had been building within him for the last few years that desperately needed an outlet: the symbolic drawings of the *Ishnesses*, his experimentation with language invention, the profound effect of his encounter with the names Éarendel and Middle-earth, were all signs that the burgeoning creativity of his mythopoetic imagination was rising to the surface of his consciousness. The brotherly container provided by the immortal four, by the TCBS, seems to have given Tolkien permission to enter fully into the world of Middle-earth, and to write down the stories that he was discovering. Tolkien said that he felt that "the TCBS had been granted some spark of fire—certainly as a body if not singly—that was destined to kindle a new light, or, what is the same thing, rekindle an old light in the world."[22] The

---

21 Tolkien, *Letters*, 10.
22 Tolkien, *Letters*, 10.

four young men felt they were in some way destined for greatness. But the First World War intervened cruelly, and the promise of that greatness was cut short.

After completing his degree at Oxford, Tolkien enlisted with the Lancashire Fusiliers and was appointed as a signalman due to his skill with language and codes. This appointment shielded him from the direct harm that befell so many thousands of other young men. Tolkien was present at the devastating Battle of the Somme, but he was not engaged directly in the action. Yet it was in this battle that the lights of both Gilson and Smith were extinguished. Gilson died at the front lines on the first day of the Somme offensive, on July 1, 1916, one of 100,000 that day who marched straight into machine gun fire, their bravery overcoming the folly of their superiors' commands.[23] A fifth of all soldiers who entered No Man's Land on that single day perished, and twice as many again were wounded. The casualties were even greater the following day. For five months the Battle of the Somme surged and quailed, a failure of planning and imagination on the part of the British generals.[24] The nature of warfare had changed, and the old battle

---

23 Garth, *Tolkien and the Great War*, 152–58.
24 Paul Fussell, *The Great War and Modern Memory* (New York: Oxford UP, 2013), 13–14.

tactics no longer worked. Nearly a whole generation met their wretched demise in the mud, in the damp pits, in the horror of the trenches. The mark of this horror, this waste of life, this darkness, can be felt in the deaths, losses, and scenes of battle Tolkien describes not only in *The Lord of the Rings*, but in all his stories.

After Rob Gilson's death, the remaining three members of the TCBS were left reeling with grief, and struggled to understand their own roles in the face of this loss.[25] Were they meant to achieve their great work? Could it be done when one, and soon to be two, of their number had left the world forever? Geoffrey Smith seemed to have some intuition of the fate that also awaited him. Not long before he died, Smith sent Tolkien a letter saying:

> Death can make us loathsome and helpless as individuals, but it cannot put an end to the immortal four! . . . May God bless you, my dear John Ronald, and may you say the things I have tried to say long after I am not there to say them, if such be my lot.
>
> Yours ever,
>
> G.B.S.[26]

---

25 Garth, *Tolkien and the Great War*, 156, 176.

26 G.B. Smith, as quoted in Carpenter, *Tolkien: A Biography*, 94; Garth, *Tolkien and the Great War*, 118–19.

"May you say the things I have tried to say long after I am not there to say them." Smith had appointed Tolkien with an impossible task. How could he do justice to their loss, to their suffering? How do you say the things that your deceased friends have not been given enough time to say? Perhaps it was this mission, to carry on the moral and aesthetic vision of rekindling a new light in the world, that stoked the fire in Tolkien to bring an entire mythology into being.

Fangorn Forest

3

The Two Towers – *Book III*
From Rohan and Fangorn to Isengard

THE FELLOWSHIP HAS NOW SPLIT, its members each departing in different directions, some willingly, some by force. When we open *The Two Towers* we pick up right where the end of *The Fellowship of the Ring* left off, and this continuation of the narrative thread reminds us that *The Lord of the Rings* is not a trilogy but rather one single story, sub-divided into six books. The end of *The Fellowship of the Ring* does not come to a climax or conclusion in the way one would expect from the ending of the first volume of a real trilogy. Rather, the story remains open-ended, ready for the journey to continue. J. R. R. Tolkien never intended *The Lord of the Rings* to be a trilogy; publication costs required the separation of the books into three volumes, each published several months apart.

In the first chapter, **"The Departure of Boromir,"** we experience the loss of yet another member of the Fellowship. His final words, after admitting that he tried to take the Ring from Frodo, and that he paid for his sin with his own life, is to say: "I have failed."[1] He speaks no more after that. One can feel the tragedy of this moment, but also Tolkien's own deep pessimism coming through in these words. We can also hear in Boromir's final words the heavy weight of loss that Tolkien experienced in his life. That sense of tragedy shaped every story that came through him, even the most fantastical and enchanted of stories. This gravitas is part of what gives such depth and moral drama to the mythology of Middle-earth, and why it feels so ancient and even timeless, and yet also so resonant with the twentieth century and even our contemporary moment in history.

The beginning of *The Two Towers* takes us immediately into a world at war. We do not see the direct conflict that leads to Boromir's death and Pippin and Merry's capture, but we begin to see the complex alliances between the warring factions of Middle-earth. The story is now more political and strategic. Instead of a world of hobbits and Elves, we have now entered a world of Men—human beings—and the world of Orcs, who seem to symbolize the worst impulses and nasty underbelly of humanity.

---

[1] J.R.R. Tolkien, *The Lord of the Rings: The Two Towers* (New York: Houghton Mifflin, 2014), III, i, 404.

In the second chapter, **"The Riders of Rohan,"** the chase of the Three Hunters—Aragorn, Legolas, and Gimli—across Rohan shows Aragorn's immense skill as a tracker, able to read the most subtle signs of the landscape and even to listen to the Earth itself. We also see his humility. He feels his every choice has gone amiss since they passed through the Argonath, the two great statues of his ancestors that tower over the Great River. That is significant because it is upon crossing the threshold to his own realm of Gondor that Aragorn feels his choices have all been wrong. He also speaks of how the true Quest lies with Frodo, and that their own task is "but a small matter in the great deeds of this time."[2] He does not overvalue his own part in this history, even though he is a figure descended from kings.

As the Three Hunters run across the verdant, fertile plains of Rohan, we learn something interesting about Legolas and about Elvish consciousness: he is able to rest his mind in the "strange paths of elvish dreams" even while he is walking open-eyed in the light of this world.[3] This single line tells us much about the difference between Elves and humans. They are able to be in the world of dreams in a waking state, and from such

---

2 Tolkien, *The Two Towers*, III, ii, 416.
3 Tolkien, *The Two Towers*, III, ii, 419.

wanderings are rejuvenated in the same way sleep rejuvenates us. This hearkens back to Gimli's comment to Legolas on the Great River when he says that for Elves memory seems to be more like waking than the faded images with which we mortals are left. Why is that? My speculation is because Elves, as immortal beings bound forever to this world, do not have the escape of death that mortals are afforded. They must find escape and rest in some other way—and this is by, in some sense, altering their consciousness and entering into an otherworld while still awake. Elves can almost be understood as an embodiment of what it means to be in a non-ordinary state of consciousness. They are an incarnation of the dreamworld, a form of living memory themselves.

When the Three Hunters encounter the éored of the Rohirrim, led by Éomer, we learn a little of the history of the Rohirrim. Their people were originally from the north of Middle-earth, but they were led south by Eorl the Young to aid Gondor in the fight against Sauron. Their language and culture is akin to the Anglo-Saxon language and culture beloved by Tolkien. The name Eorl is from a line of Old English poetry; other names such as Éomer and Éowyn, as well as the term éored for a troop of horses, all stem from the word *eoh* meaning "horse."[4]

---

4 Shippey, *The Road to Middle-Earth*, 20–21.

Tolkien even embedded linguistic changes in the history of the Rohirrim itself. For example, before Eorl the Young brought the Rohirrim from the North to inhabit the Gondorian plains of Rohan, the names of Rohirric leaders had Gothic origins: Vidugavia, Vidumavi, Marhwini.[5] Only after they enter into allegiance with Gondor do the Rohirrim take on Anglo-Saxon names. Both the words *ent* and *wose* appeared in Old English poetry, and in Middle-earth the Rohirrim are appropriately situated between the Entish woods of Fangorn, and the Druadan Forest in which the Woses dwell to the South.[6]

When Aragorn reveals his lineage to Éomer, Legolas sees a white flame above Aragorn's brow for a moment. This fleeting image recalls the vision that the four hobbits had upon the barrow-downs, of a lineage of men with swords and the last with a star on his brow. Éomer's response is to say that "Dreams and legends spring to life out of the grass."[7] When they describe the hobbits, or halflings, Éomer says that they are only a little people from old songs and children's tales out of the North. He asks: "Do we walk in legends

---

5   Shippey, *The Road to Middle-Earth*, 15.

6   Shippey, *The Road to Middle-Earth*, 131.

7   Tolkien, *The Two Towers*, III, ii, 423.

or on the green earth in daylight?"[8] King Théoden has a similar response several chapters later, in the chapter "The Road to Isengard," when he sees the Ents for the first time. He says: "Out of the shadows of legend I begin a little to understand the marvel of the trees."[9] Ents and halflings have only been remembered in songs taught to children, easily dismissed or forgotten. Does this not sound like the dismissal of fairy-stories in our own time? Even in Middle-earth, human beings forget that there is more to the world than what takes place in their insular, disenchanted culture. What can this teach us? What about the world have we dismissed as only a fairy-tale, something that is just imaginary or only a fantasy? When Éomer asks, "Do we walk in legends or on the green earth in daylight?" Aragorn says in response, "A man may do both."[10] He reminds Éomer that the green Earth itself is a mighty matter of legend, just as we might do to remember that the doorways to Faërie can perhaps best be found out in the forests, the meadows, by the sea, and the great expanses of nature. Aragorn also reminds Éomer that it is those who will come afterwards who will make the legends of their

---

8 Tolkien, *The Two Towers*, III, ii, 424.
9 Tolkien, *The Two Towers*, III, viii, 536.
10 Tolkien, *The Two Towers*, III, ii, 424.

time. This is one of several self-reflexive moments in *The Lord of the Rings*, when the characters know they are in a story that is being told.

The Three Hunters come to the edge of Fangorn forest, and here we learn that it is akin to the Old Forest in which Tom Bombadil dwells. The two forests are vestiges of the Elder Days, older even than the Firstborn, the Elves who first wandered the Earth. But it is through the eyes of the hobbits Pippin and Merry that we first see beneath the eaves of this great woodland realm.

However, before coming to Fangorn, the captive hobbits make their horrific journey with the orcs across the plains of Rohan in chapter three, "**The Uruk-Hai.**" The tensions between the different factions are intriguing: there are the powerful Uruk-hai of Isengard, who can withstand the light of the Sun. There are the orcs from Lugbúrz, the orcish name for Barad-Dûr, the Dark Tower in Mordor. And there are the orcs from the Misty Mountains, who want to seek vengeance for the passage of the Fellowship through the Mines of Moria.

What is so striking about this chapter, which we see through Pippin's eyes, is the way Pippin comes into his own as he recognizes he needs to rescue Merry and himself. The "Fool of a Took" is far more capable than one might have at first realized. Often it is only in a dire situation that our greatest courage and cleverness are able to emerge in response. When Pippin, and then Merry as he catches on, begin tempting the Mordor orc Grishnákh with the Ring—without, importantly, ever naming it—there is almost a seduction taking place. Pippin's imitation of Gollum in this scene is also curious, especially since that is what signifies to Grishnákh that Pippin is indeed referring to the Ring. Was Grishnákh present at the torture of Gollum in Mordor many years before? Or is the term "my precious" a common phrase for mortals caught in the snares of the Ring? Bilbo called the Ring "my precious" seventeen years before in Bag End when he was struggling to leave it behind for Frodo. Whatever the reason, it is the words "my precious" that tip Grishnákh off and seduce him into Pippin's game.[11]

The chapter concludes with a description of the final stand of Uglúk, the fierce captain of the Uruk-hai, in sword to sword combat with Éomer, who finally slays him. Tolkien never leaves a thread untied, and we can feel the satisfaction that such an evil opponent was not taken down by a stray arrow or by an unnamed rider, but rather by Éomer himself, leader of the company and nephew to the king of Rohan.

11 Tolkien, *The Two Towers*, III, iii, 445.

The fourth chapter, **"Treebeard,"** introduces us to perhaps one of the most fantastical beings in contemporary literature, and yet a being who has deep roots in legend and myth as the green man, or as spirits and dryads of the forest. Yet despite these mythic roots, Ents are both unique and yet oddly familiar: how many of us have seen faces or arms and long-fingered hands on trees and wondered if they could move or what they might have to say? Who has not wished that the trees might rise in their own defense, especially when we humans who love trees find we cannot protect all the great forests that we love? When Treebeard is asked which side he is on, he gives a telling answer: "I am not altogether on anybody's *side*, because nobody is altogether on my *side*, if you understand me: nobody cares for the woods as I care for them."[12] We hear in Treebeard's words the same moral ambiguity we felt when the hobbits traversed the Old Forest: there are more than two sides in Middle-earth, more than simply a struggle between good and evil. There is the will of nature, and the wills of the many different peoples of Middle-earth. It is not always clear on whose side we are meant to be in any given conflict.[13]

---

12 Tolkien, *The Two Towers*, III, iv, 461.
13 Flieger, "Taking the Part of the Trees," 262–74.

The culture of Ents is one of song and language, of names, of memory, and most importantly, the slow passage of time. The Elvish name that Treebeard hums to himself to describe Lothlórien—*Laurelindórenan lindelorendor malinornélion ornemalin*—translates as "Land of the Valley of Singing Gold, singing dreamland, mallorn golden/yellow tree, bearing yellow flowers."[14] And the long name that Treebeard gives to Fangorn forest—*Taurelilómëa-tumbalemorna Tumbaletaurëa Lómëanor*—translates as "there is a black shadow in the deep dales of the forest."[15]

The Great Darkness to which Treebeard refers is the shadow of Morgoth, the first Dark Lord, who for a time overtook most of Middle-earth while the world was still young. The newborn Elves, who were waking up the trees and learning to speak with them, fled to the Undying Lands in the West over the Sea, as Treebeard says, or hid themselves throughout Middle-earth. This creates the great sundering of the Elves, which leads to the many different Elven kindreds who speak a diversity of languages. Only the Elves who undertook the journey

---

14 Tolkien, *The Two Towers*, III, iv, 456; Noel, *The Languages of Tolkien's Middle-Earth*, 40.

15 Tolkien, *The Two Towers*, III, iv, 456; Noel, *The Languages of Tolkien's Middle-Earth*, 40.

to pass over the Sea and behold the blessed light of the Undying Lands are called the Eldar, or the High Elves.[16] The Elves who remained in Middle-earth have many other names: the Sindar or the Grey Elves, the Sylvan Elves or Wood Elves, the Moriquendi or the Dark Elves. There are many different kinds of Elves in the world, although we only learn about a few of them in *The Lord of the Rings*. *The Silmarillion* is concerned mostly with the doings of the High Elves, particularly the Noldor.

Treebeard's song about the seasons speaks of many places that were located in Beleriand, the western region of the continent of Middle-earth, which drowned at the end of the First Age: Tasarinan, Ossiriand, Neldoreth, Dorthonion, are all names of places that are prominent in *The Silmarillion*, in the tales of the First Age. Thus we learn how very old Treebeard is.

When Treebeard speaks about the wizards, he says that they came after the Great Ships came over the Sea. Here he is referring to the Númenoreans, Aragorn's ancestors who came to Middle-earth by ship throughout the Second Age. Treebeard says he does not know if the wizards came with the ships, but I can tell you now

---

16 For a book exploring the symbolic meaning of the sundering of the Elves and their relationship to language and light, see Verlyn Flieger, *Splintered Light: Logos and Language in Tolkien's World*, 2nd edition (Kent, OH: The Kent State UP, 2002).

that they did not—the wizards, also called the Istari, came from the Blessed Realm itself, from the Uttermost West, and they were sent by the Valar to aid in the struggle against Sauron. The wizards are Maiar, spirits of the same kind but lesser order as the Valar. They were all originally Ainur before the world was sung into being during the *Ainulindalë*. There were five wizards sent to Middle-earth: Saruman the White, Gandalf the Grey, Radagast the Brown, and two blue wizards of which we know nothing further. They may have gone East, and there are rumors they may even have joined Sauron. But, just like the cats of Queen Berúthiel, Tolkien admitted he did not know more about the two blue wizards. Alas, the same must be said of the Entwives: no one knows what became of them, and no story tells of their fate. It is one of the few threads left untied in this mythology.

After the Entmoot, as the Ents march to war against Isengard, Treebeard reflects: "likely enough that we are going to *our* doom: the last march of the Ents. But if we stayed at home and did nothing, doom would find us anyway, sooner or later."[17] The story of *The Lord of the Rings*, although filled with violence and battles, is a story of defense—defending homes and families and

---

17   Tolkien, *The Two Towers*, III, iv, 475.

the diverse cultures that are shaped by the landscape itself. Doom finds one anyway if we choose to do nothing. So is it not better to rise to meet it instead?

For a story of war and conflict, much time is spent in describing the stillness. This chapter ends not with the Ents' attack on Isengard, but rather with the silence before the storm. That last line of the chapter always gives me chills, when Treebeard says: "Night lies over Isengard."[18]

When we come to chapter five, **"The White Rider,"** we encounter someone we did not expect to meet. When one reads *The Lord of the Rings* for the first time, this moment is pivotal. I have spoken to many people about their first experiences of reading *The Lord of the Rings*, especially if they first read it at a younger age, and the devastation that is felt when Gandalf is lost in Moria, and the ecstatic surprise at his return, is immense. Yet for those who know what to look for, there are hints of Gandalf's return throughout the intervening story. For example, Aragorn sees an eagle from Amon Hen, the Hill of Seeing in the chapter "The Departure of Boromir," and Legolas sees that same eagle flying above Rohan in the chapter "The Riders of Rohan." This is Gwaihir, circling the lands above the members of the Fellowship.

---

18 Tolkien, *The Two Towers*, III, iv, 476.

Most importantly, we can remember the Voice that strove with the Eye at the end of *The Fellowship of the Ring* when Frodo sat upon the Hill of Seeing. The voice told Frodo to take the Ring off, and called him a fool. "Fool, take it off!"[19] Who so liberally uses the word "fool"? Calling Pippin a fool in Moria for dropping a stone down the open hole in the floor, and saying to the company before he plunged into the abyss below the Bridge of Khazad-dûm, "Fly, you fools!"[20] Gandalf. He even refers to the Quest of the Ring as appearing folly in "The Council of Elrond," and says that folly will be their cloak to hide their errand from the Dark Lord.[21] Gandalf was the Voice who strove against Sauron, while Frodo was wearing the Ring and caught in the balance between the two voices and wills present there. Gandalf was the Voice telling Frodo to take off the Ring.

Gandalf's presence still permeates the story, even after his fall with the Balrog. In Frodo's vision in the Mirror of Galadriel, he sees a figure walking down a long, grey road who reminds him of Gandalf.[22] But before he calls out the wizard's name, he sees that his robes

---

19 Tolkien, *The Fellowship of the Ring*, II, x, 392.

20 Tolkien, *The Fellowship of the Ring*, II, v, 322.

21 Tolkien, *The Fellowship of the Ring*, II, ii, 262.

22 Tolkien, *The Fellowship of the Ring*, II, vii, 354.

are white, and he wonders if in fact he is looking at Saruman. We learn that it is Galadriel who clothed Gandalf in white after his resurrection, and because of the nature of Galadriel's mirror, she too would have seen the same vision Frodo did in that moment. In terms of the timeline, when Frodo saw this vision aligns exactly with the day that Gandalf returned to his body and was rescued from the mountaintop by the eagle Gwaihir. Galadriel sent the eagle to look for Gandalf, likely because of the vision she saw that day in her mirror.

When Gandalf hears the tale from Aragorn—and is it not curious to note how many times throughout this story the tale of each character's adventure is told again and again to others?—his response to Boromir's death is noteworthy. Gandalf says that Galadriel had warned him Boromir was in peril, but that he escaped in the end. One would not think of Boromir's death as being an escape, but it actually is. There is a fate worse than death in Gandalf's eyes: falling temptation to the Ring and betraying the Fellowship and the Quest. By turning his energy to defending Pippin and Merry, Boromir was saved from that fate, and he died as himself, uncorrupted in the end by the Ring.

Gandalf's tale of his own ordeal evokes powerful images: the deep water at the base of the abyss, the foundations of stone of the mountains. "Far, far below the deepest delvings of the Dwarves, the world is gnawed by nameless things. Even Sauron knows them not. They are older than he."[23] *The world is gnawed by nameless things.* The Endless Stair, Durin's Tower—these are such primordial images, the wedding of mountain rock and the contours of sculpted architecture.

We learn nothing about where Gandalf's spirit goes when he strays out of thought and time, nor who it is who sends him back for a brief time, until his task is done. We can presume it is the Valar, the Powers of the World.

When Gandalf and Shadowfax, and the Three Hunters come south to Edoras and the Hall of Meduseld in the sixth chapter, "**The King of the Golden Hall**," we have entered a world that echoes the great Anglo-Saxon poem *Beowulf*, which Tolkien translated at one time in his life. Tolkien's analysis of that poem changed the scholarly discourse on *Beowulf*, taking the poem as a work of art and a product of the literary imagination, not just a medieval artifact to be dissected for historical facts. If you are interested in Tolkien's analysis and defense of that poem, I recommend his essay "Beowulf: The Monsters and the Critics."[24]

---

23 Tolkien, *The Two Towers*, III, v, 490.
24 J.R.R. Tolkien, "Beowulf: The Monsters and the Critics," in *The Monsters and the Critics*, ed. Christopher Tolkien, (London: HarperCollins): 5–48.

We see Gandalf's new power and authority as he draws Théoden from the poisoned dream into which Saruman's servant Gríma, the Wormtongue, has lured him. And here too we meet Éowyn for the first time, the white lady of Rohan, niece to the king and sister to Éomer. The connection made between Éowyn and Aragorn is only subtly described, as is Tolkien's way when it comes to romance, and yet there is a feeling of fate here, something kindled between them both.

We learn too that it was because of desire for Éowyn that Wormtongue betrayed his people and became a spy for Saruman. And we learn also that the people of Rohan love her, and trust her as a leader. When Théoden makes the choice to ride to battle, the Rohirrim ask for Éowyn to lead them in his stead. Such a thought does not even occur to Théoden, but it is more than obvious to his people. When the King and his warriors depart, the final image at the end of the chapter is of Éowyn standing still, alone before the doors of the silent house. None of these images are wasted in Tolkien's prose. The silence, the stillness, the loneliness, are all a part of Éowyn's story.

The original plan for Théoden and his riders was to go to the Fords of Isen, south of Isengard, to aid the Rohirrim there already fighting against Saruman. Because of this westward fight, Wormtongue had argued to Théoden that Éomer should not ride north to encounter the raiding orcs who had captured Merry and Pippin. Because of Éomer's disobedience, he had briefly been imprisoned at Edoras. Already the fight is taking place on multiple fronts in Rohan.

In chapter seven, "**Helm's Deep**," the company of the king learn from a messenger that the Rohirrim who were at the Fords of Isen had been overtaken and scattered, and that Erkenbrand of Westfold had brought all the men he could to Helm's Deep. Gandalf advises Théoden and his riders to make for Helm's Deep as quickly as possible, because he has seen or somehow perceived that Erkenbrand and his people were also scattered by the hosts of Saruman. Gandalf sets out immediately upon Shadowfax to gather these lost Rohirrim and bring them safely to Helm's Deep.

The Hornburg inside Helm's Deep was not built by the Rohirrim, but was built thousands of years before by the Númenoreans. The Rohirrim have only been in Rohan for five hundred years, a mere season when compared to the lives of Elves or Ents, or even the history of Gondor.

There are about a thousand men to defend the Hornburg, plus however many rode out from Edoras with Théoden. When Gimli and Legolas are standing upon the wall of the stronghold, Gimli mentions his weariness and need for sleep. Thus, it seems worth mentioning here how long it has been since they last slept: the Three Hunters slept by the eaves of Fangorn, and then the following morning encountered Gandalf within the forest itself. The four of them then rode south through the rest of that day and into the night, and only had a few hours of sleep before riding on to Edoras, arriving a little after sunrise. Gandalf then persuaded Théoden to come forth and ride to battle all in one day, and the company arrives at Helm's Deep at nightfall. In the three days prior to this, the Three Hunters were running on foot all the way across Rohan, from the Great River Anduin to Fangorn. So they must be weary indeed. And now battle lies before them, and they fight all through the long night.

The symbolism in the outer world mirrors how events unfold in the battle: the long dark night, the heavy storm, the flashing lightning. Aragorn comes forth to look for the dawn, and it is with the light of a new day that new hope is brought to the defenders of the Hornburg. Light springs into the sky and night departs as Théoden and Aragorn ride forth to battle. Gandalf is illuminated in the rising Sun as he returns with the host of Erkenbrand. These patterns of storm and sunlight continue throughout the story, and often foretell what will unfold in the narrative.

During the whole journey in the chapter "**The Road to Isengard**," Gandalf only offers hints of what he knows is unfolding in the Wizard's Vale. He does not correct misconceptions, from Théoden or anyone else. He seems intent only on his errand, and keeps all knowledge and explanations to himself unless absolutely necessary. His silence allows the truth to unfold before the eyes of the riders, and the reader, in the living moment, rather than through lengthy explanation. Gandalf shows the truth, rather than asking others to trust his words. How different he shows himself to be than Saruman in this way.

When Théoden and the riders first see the hobbits Merry and Pippin, Théoden remarks that some among the Rohirrim call them the Holbytlan. When Tolkien wrote the legendary first sentence of *The Hobbit*, "In a hole in the ground there lived a hobbit," he did not even know what a hobbit was—but he soon set about finding out.[25] As a philologist, he did this linguistically: he connected the word "hobbit" to the Old English word *hol-bytla*, which translates as "hole-dweller."[26]

---

25 J.R.R. Tolkien, *The Hobbit: Or There and Back Again* (Boston: Houghton Mifflin Company, 1991), 9; Carpenter, *Tolkien: A Biography*, 175.

26 Shippey, *The Road to Middle-Earth*, 66.

Thus, Théoden's Rohirric name for the hobbits is actually the Anglo-Saxon name for "hole-dweller." That the Rohirrim have tales of hobbits in their folklore, unlike other Men or races of Middle-earth, indicates that there may be some distant kinship between the two: Big People and Little People, both descended out of the northern lands of Middle-earth. The end of this chapter perfectly captures the clashing of the interior world of the Shire and the hobbits with the grand exterior world of Middle-earth: "So that is the King of Rohan!" said Pippin in an undertone. "A fine old fellow. Very polite."[27]

Chapter nine, **"Flotsam and Jetsam,"** is almost entirely a story within a story, with Pippin and Merry recounting their tale of the Ents' assault upon Isengard. So much occurs in just nine days at this stage in the story—very different than in *The Fellowship of the Ring*. I find it interesting how some tales are meant to be retold, while others are experienced in the unfolding. But in both cases there is an oral history here that is slowly being recorded, eventually to be put down into *The Red Book of Westmarch*.

The title "Flotsam and Jetsam" has a nautical source, as both terms refer to kinds of marine debris.

---

27 Tolkien, *The Two Towers*, III, viii, 545.

Flotsam is debris floating in the water that was not deliberately thrown overboard, often as the result of an accident or a shipwreck. The word flotsam derives from the French word *floter*, meaning "to float." Jetsam refers to debris that was intentionally thrown overboard by the crew of a ship in distress, usually as a means to lighten the ship's load. Jetsam is a shortened word for "jettison." So Tolkien's use of these terms refers to the debris found by Merry and Pippin floating in the waters around Isengard, after misfortune had befallen Saruman. In some ways everything the hobbits find is flotsam, but there is one important item of jetsam thrown from Orthanc in the following chapter: the Palantír.

The outcome of the conversation in chapter ten, **"The Voice of Saruman,"** can be summed up in Gandalf's remark: "Often does hatred hurt itself!"[28] Indeed, we can remember this for other moments later in this story, when we see what evil hatred works upon itself.

The final chapter of Book III, **"The Palantir,"** sets in motion with a new rapidity the next stage in the journey, and it ties together the current moment with lore and artifacts from the earliest days of Middle-earth.

---

28 Tolkien, *The Two Towers*, III, x, 571.

Once more the plans change suddenly: instead of Théoden and his men riding back to the Golden Hall in Edoras, they are now going straight on to Dunharrow, although first with a brief stop back at Helm's Deep. Just as when Théoden planned to go to the Fords of Isen but then turned aside to Helm's Deep, here too the plans are altered based on new information discerned by Gandalf. While this makes the plot more complex, it also reflects the changing realities of many moving factions of people across the land.

When Pippin picks up the Palantír he is infected by desire for it, in a way similar to one who handles the One Ring. This is an artifact of great power. The Palantír—which means "far-seeing" in Elvish—as Aragorn says, comes from the treasury of Elendil and is an heirloom of Númenor. But the seven Seeing Stones have a history older even than Númenor—they were said to have been forged by Fëanor himself, the great Elvish craftsman who also made the three Silmarils. The Palantíri were set throughout the kingdoms of Gondor and Arnor in strategic positions, so that the entire kingdom was united in sight and communication.

As Gandalf rides through the night with Pippin, he recites several lines from the Rhymes of Lore:

*Tall ships and tall kings
Three times three,
What brought they from the foundered land
Over the flowing sea?
Seven stars and seven stones
And one white tree.*[29]

These are the legends behind the founding of Gondor, telling of how Elendil and his two sons Isildur and Anárion, named for the Moon—*Isil*—and the Sun—*Anar*—came to Middle-earth riding the waves of the storm that sunk Númenor. The numbers in the poem echo the same numbers as in the Ring poem that opens *The Lord of the Rings*. Instead of three rings for the Elvenkings, seven for the Dwarf lords, nine for mortal men, and one for the Dark Lord, we have three kings and nine ships—three times three as the poem says—and they bring seven stars and seven stones, and one white tree. These numbers are sacred, significant, and bear the mark of fate upon them.

Where did these lines come from? This remarkable passage comes from one of Tolkien's letters, a portion of which I have quoted previously, in which he describes his experience of discovering the unfolding narrative of *The Lord of the Rings*:

29 Tolkien, *The Two Towers*, III, xi, 583.

> I met a lot of things on the way that astonished me. Tom Bombadil I knew already; but I had never been to Bree. Strider sitting in the corner at the inn was a shock, and I had no more idea who he was than had Frodo. The Mines of Moria had been a mere name; and of Lothlórien no word had reached my mortal ears till I came there. Far away I knew there were the Horse-lords on the confines of an ancient Kingdom of Men, but Fangorn Forest was an unforeseen adventure. I had never heard of the House of Eorl nor of the Stewards of Gondor. Most disquieting of all, Saruman had never been revealed to me, and I was as mystified as Frodo at Gandalf's failure to appear on September 22. I knew nothing of the *Palantíri*, though the moment the Orthanc-stone was cast from the window, I recognized it, and knew the meaning of the "rhyme of lore" that had been running in my mind: *seven stars and seven stones and one white tree*. These rhymes and names will crop up; but they do not always explain themselves.[30]

Gandalf says even he is tempted to look into the Palantír, to see what he can see. He longs to look back into the deeps of time, to see the great Elvish city Tirion

---

30 Tolkien, *Letters*, 216–17.

the Fair in the Undying Lands, to perceive the hand and mind of Fëanor at work as he made the Silmarils that captured the light of the Two Trees of Valinor in their unbreakable crystalline encasing. These objects of power interconnect so intimately: the Silmarils and the Palantíri both made by Fëanor, the Great Rings made by his grandson Celebrimbor. The objects in some sense drive the story, and the people come and go from the tale: *The Silmarillion*, *The Lord of the Rings*—objects are central to the titles of these tales, and they pull the many people into their orbit.

We now leave for a time the outer story of *The Lord of the Rings*: the battles and armies, politics and plots, the kings and counsellors. We turn away from the tales of Aragorn, Legolas, and Gimli, Gandalf the White, Merry and Pippin, Fangorn, Rohan, and Isengard. As Book III comes to a close the story next delves inward, to the true Quest.

Interlude

The Languages of Middle-Earth

IN CONJUNCTION WITH THE DRAWINGS Tolkien made in *The Book of Ishness*, and alongside his first stories of Middle-earth, Tolkien was also beginning to develop his Elvish lexicons: complex word lists tracing the etymology of particular words to their invented roots. The lexicons are remarkably sophisticated, clearly the product of an individual who understood the structure and evolution of language from the inside. Tolkien wished to compose languages as others composed symphonies.[1] The first lexicons—for the languages Qenya (later Quenya, or High Elvish) and Goldogrin (which would later evolve into Sindarin, or Grey Elvish)—were housed in two intensely revised little notebooks that were organized according to root words. As Tolkien noted at the beginning of the Qenya lexicon, root words "are not words in use at all, but serve as an elucidation of the words grouped together and a connection

1   Carpenter, *Tolkien: A Biography*, 44.

between them."[2] Tolkien was tracing particular Elvish words back to their root source, rather than beginning with the root and creating words branching out from there. Tolkien's son Christopher made this interesting observation: "it seems clear that the word was 'there,' so to speak, but its etymology remained to be certainly defined, and not vice versa."[3] I cannot help but notice the way Christopher's description of the Elvish word already being "there" echoes J.R.R. Tolkien's sense when writing his stories that he was "recording what was already 'there,' somewhere," as he said in one of his letters.[4] Tolkien often spoke of his languages as being "invented," but as the philologist Tom Shippey has pointed out, by a lovely twist of etymological fate the root of the word "invention" is the Latin *invenire*, meaning "to find."[5] One has the sense that Tolkien's invention of languages, like the writing of his stories, was a process of initial discovery followed by detailed elaboration.

Tolkien rarely spoke in plain terms about the origins of the words in his invented languages, even

---

2 Tolkien, *The Book of Lost Tales: Part I*, "Appendix," 246.
3 Christopher Tolkien, ed., *The Book of Lost Tales: Part I*, "Appendix," 246.
4 Tolkien, *Letters*, 145.
5 Shippey, *Road to Middle-Earth*, 25.

though such language-sculpting was a passion of his throughout the many decades of his life. He would steal away hours from his other work and obligations so that he might "niggle" with his languages. He was fine tuning the relationships between the words and the phonetic shifts that allowed the invented words to evolve from their root sounds.[6] Interestingly, the words themselves often came with a known meaning, and Tolkien would delight in discovering the "phonetic fitness" of the words in relation to what the words symbolized.[7] But what was the actual origin of the words? Where did they come from? Was Tolkien just making them up?

Couched within the fabula of a number of his stories, Tolkien describes the experience of linguistic discovery and the recognition that would come with hearing certain words and intuitively knowing the meanings associated with them. His two unfinished stories *The Lost Road* and *The Notion Club Papers* both contain characters who speak about languages "coming through,"[8]

---

6 Tolkien, "The Notion Club Papers," 240.

7 J.R.R. Tolkien, "A Secret Vice," in *The Monsters and the Critics*, ed. Christopher Tolkien, (London: HarperCollins), 211.

8 J.R.R. Tolkien, "The Lost Road," in *The History of Middle-Earth: The Lost Road and Other Writings*, vol. 5, ed. Christopher Tolkien, (New York: Houghton Mifflin, 2010), 41.

or the hearing of "ghost words."[9] Tolkien never publicly used such phrases to describe his own personal experiences, but there is an uncanny similarity between the words and meanings described as "coming through" in these two stories and many of the words recorded in Tolkien's early lexicons. Nonetheless, simply because Tolkien included descriptions of certain experiences in his fiction does not mean he shared in such experiences himself.

As an example, in *The Lost Road* the young character Alboin Errol—who has many of Tolkien's same interests and proclivities—shares several words from two different languages that have been coming through to him, languages that he calls *Eressëan*, or *Elf-latin*, and *Beleriandic*. In the former language the word for "tree" is *alda*, while in the second language the word for "tree" is both *galadh* and *orn*. The word *lōmë* means "night," and can be found in the compound word *lōmelindë*, which translates as "nightingale." The words for "Sun" and "Moon" in *Eressëan* are *Anar* and *Isil*, while in *Beleriandic* they have the slightly different names *Anor* and *Ithil*.[10] Likewise, in the later story *The Notion Club Papers*, the character Arry Lowdham describes some

---

9 Tolkien, "The Notion Club Papers," 238.
10 Tolkien, "The Lost Road," 41.

of the first "ghost words" that came to him. This is Lowdham's speech to his fellow Notion Club Members:

> Yes, *lōme* is "night" (but *not* "darkness") and *lōmelinde* is "a nightingale": I feel sure of that. In the second language it is *dūmh*, later *dū*; and *duilin*. I refer them to a Primitive Western *dōmi, dōmilindē*. *Alda* means a "tree"—it was one of the earliest certain words I got—and *orne* when smaller and more slender like a birch or rowan; in the second language I find *galađ*, and *orn* (plural *yrn*): I refer them to *galadā*, and *ornē* (plural *ornei*). Sometimes the forms are more similar: the Sun and Moon, for instance, appear as *Anār, Isil* beside *Anaur* (later *Anor*) and *Ithil*. I liked first the one language and then the other in different linguistic moods, but the older seemed always the more august, somehow, the more, I don't know . . . liturgical, monumental: I used to call it the Elven-latin; and the other seemed more resonant with the loss and regret of these shores of exile.[11]

Tolkien uses the same words as examples in both *The Lost Road* and *The Notion Club Papers* to illustrate his point about two distinct but related languages "coming

11 Tolkien, "The Notion Club Papers," 302.

through." If you compare the words used in *The Lord of the Rings* and *The Silmarillion*, you will discover that these languages are in fact Tolkien's two Elvish languages of Quenya and Sindarin, which he began developing in 1915 or earlier.[12] Quenya is the Elven-latin, while Sindarin is the language that carries the sense of poignant nostalgia and loss, which the character Lowdham describes.

The scholar Lance Owens has suggested that *The Notion Club Papers* may be the story in which Tolkien most explicitly discusses his own experiences in relation to language, imagination, and story.[13] Speaking through Arry Lowdham, Tolkien describes how the words that belonged to the two related ghost-languages were encountered:

> It was a long time before I began to note them down, and use them for the language I was amusing myself by "making up." They did not fit, or rather they took control and bent that language to their own style. In fact it became difficult to tell which were my invented words and which were

---

12 Christopher Tolkien, ed., *The Book of Lost Tales: Part I*, "Appendix," 246–47.

13 Lance S. Owens, "Jung and Tolkien: The Hermeneutics of Vision," (Lecture hosted by the Philosophy, Cosmology, and Consciousness Forum, presented at the California Institute of Integral Studies, San Francisco, CA, 23 October 2015).

> the ghost-words; indeed I've a notion that "invention" gradually played a smaller and smaller part.[14]

One cannot help but wonder if Tolkien is referring to his own experiences, and that perhaps he too heard ghost words that became the basis for his language creation. In *The Notion Club Papers*, Lowdham goes on to elucidate the difference between inventing languages and the ghost words that would come through of their own accord:

> When you're just inventing, the pleasure or fun is in the moment of invention; but as you are the master your whim is law, and you may want to have the fun all over again, fresh. You're liable to be for ever niggling, altering, refining, wavering, according to your linguistic mood and to the changes of taste. It is not in the least like that with my ghost-words. They came through made: sound and sense already conjoined. I can no more niggle with them than I can alter the sound or the sense of the word *polis* in Greek. Many of my ghost-words have been repeated, over and over again, down the years. Nothing changes but occasionally my spelling. They don't change. They endure,

14 Tolkien, "The Notion Club Papers," 302.

unaltered, unalterable by me. In other words they have the effect and taste of real languages.[15]

Many of the words that Tolkien calls "ghost words" in *The Lost Road* and *The Notion Club Papers* are indeed words that he used over and over again, throughout his many years of writing the stories of Middle-earth. Except for minor changes in spelling, Tolkien repeatedly incorporated these words into the names of people and places, as well as in the Elvish poetry and dialogue spoken throughout the stories. For example, the Sindarin word *orn* can be found in the name "Aragorn," which translates as "Lord of the Tree." The name Aragorn is from the root words *ar*, meaning "high," "noble," or "royal," and *orn*, meaning "tree."[16] The other Sindarin word for "tree," *galadh*, can be found in the name of the city of *mallorn* trees at the heart of Lothlórien, Caras *Galadh*on, and in the name of the Elvish people of that realm, the *Galadh*rim. Just a note: Galadhrim and Galadriel are not related. *Galadh* means tree, while *galad* means light. *Galad* is also in the name Gil-galad.

The names for the Sun and Moon can be found in the original names for the two towers in the realm of

---

15 Tolkien, "The Notion Club Papers," 240.
16 Noel, *Languages of Tolkien's Middle-Earth*, 114, 113, 181.

Gondor: Minas *Anor*, that would one day be renamed Minas Tirith—the Tower of Guard—and Minas *Ithil*, that would fall into the hands of the Enemy and become the haunted stronghold of Minas Morgul—the Tower of Dark Sorcery.

Each name has a history and is made up of component words that can be translated. These translations have a meaning within the world of Middle-earth, but they also have different meanings connected to languages of the primary world. Coming back to the example of the name "Aragorn," his name carries philological meaning not only in Sindarin, but also in Old English. As the literary scholar David Lyle Jeffrey observed: "The first syllable, *ar*, is one of the most richly meaningful monosyllabic words in the Old English language" with meanings as diverse as "honor," "glory," "favor," and "grace."[17] The second two syllables, which Jeffrey takes together as *agorn*, can perhaps allude to Old English *agan*, meaning "to possess," or *agangan*, with the many meanings "to pass by unnoticed," "to surpass," "to travel quickly," "to come forth," or "to come to pass."[18] Each

---

17 David Lyle Jeffrey, "Tolkien as Philologist," in *Tolkien and the Invention of Myth*, ed. Jane Chance, (Lexington: The University Press of Kentucky, 2004), 71.

18 Jeffrey, "Tolkien as Philologist," 71.

of these Old English translations, with which Tolkien would have been quite familiar, has a certain bearing on Aragorn's character and destiny. "Each name," Jeffrey writes, "may be perceived as metonymic—a miniature myth, a poem, a story in itself."[19]

Interestingly though, Tolkien could also be quite resistant to certain interpretations of the names and languages of Middle-earth. He often denied the phonetic correlations to known languages. In a letter to an inquirer who had asked about the nomenclature, Tolkien wrote: "I remain puzzled, and indeed sometimes irritated, by many of the guesses at the 'sources' of the nomenclature, and theories or fancies concerning hidden meanings."[20] A frequent example he found himself refuting was the association of the name *Sauron* with the Greek word *saur, sauro*, meaning "lizard." The origin of the name Sauron is the Sindarin root *saur*, meaning "detestable," "abominable," or "abhorrent," as previously mentioned.[21] Perhaps Tolkien felt resistance to such linguistic associations because he had received many of the Sindarin or Quenya names as ghost

---

19 Jeffrey, "Tolkien as Philologist," 74.
20 Tolkien, *Letters*, 379.
21 Tolkien, *Letters*, 380; Noel, *The Languages of Tolkien's Middle-Earth*, 189.

words, accompanied by their own meanings, and felt that mistranslating them into languages of the primary world would shatter the "inner consistency of reality" in the secondary world of Middle-earth.[22] Every name, whether for person, place, or object, carries a rich history that fully resonates with the whole interwoven web of Middle-earth. Tolkien wanted Middle-earth to be seen as its own, independent mythological world.

Tolkien believed that "the making of language and mythology are related functions." He said that "to give your language an individual flavour, it must have woven into it the threads of an individual mythology.... The converse indeed is true, your language construction will *breed* a mythology."[23] This was certainly the case for Tolkien. Indeed, his recognition of this fact came just as he began writing the stories of Middle-earth: "It was just as the 1914 War burst on me that I made the discovery that 'legends' depend on the language to which they belong; but a living language depends equally on the 'legends' which it conveys by tradition."[24] Embedded within the languages themselves lived the stories of Middle-earth, as though the words were the carri-

---

22 Tolkien, *On Fairy-Stories*, 59.
23 Tolkien, "A Secret Vice," 210.
24 Tolkien, *Letters*, 231.

ers of the images and the narrative. For Tolkien, language itself seems to evoke a visionary quality, and it is intimately tied to imagination: "Language has both strengthened imagination and been freed by it," Tolkien writes. "Who shall say whether the free adjective has created images bizarre and beautiful, or the adjective been freed by strange and beautiful pictures in the mind?"[25] I would posit that both are true, and that language and image participate in one another to give birth to what Tolkien called fantasy.

---

25 Tolkien, "A Secret Vice," 219.

Emyn Muil

4

The Two Towers – *Book IV*
From the Emyn Muil to Cirith Ungol

WE HAVE NOW TURNED AWAY from the outer tale of The Lord of the Rings, from the events of the great world of human beings, of Wizards, Ents, and Orcs.[1] Now is the time to go inward, to the true Quest of this tale. This is a structure Tolkien intentionally created, moving from outer to inner. This pattern repeats in *The Return of the King* as well. Why do this? Why did Tolkien create this structure? Why not alternate chapters between different groups of people, as happens in most novels, or as Tolkien even employed in Book III when he switched from the story of Aragorn, Legolas, and Gimli, to the story of Pippin and Merry and the Ents? I believe it has to do with his desire to portray the knowledge of the characters

1 Generally, when the name of one of the peoples of Middle-earth—such as Hobbits, Elves, or Dwarves— is capitalized it refers to the people as a whole, while the lower case refers to specific groups or individuals. However, maintaining consistency is made difficult by Tolkien's own lack of consistency in his writings. Thus I accommodate where I can, and am also bound to reflect the source material, which at times evades common editing standardizations.

themselves: in the first half of *The Two Towers* we learn what is happening in the outer world alongside the different characters as their adventures proceed. In the second half of *The Two Towers* this knowledge is not available. Frodo and Sam are isolated in their story and know little outside of their immediate environment. Their story needs to be isolated from the rest, because that is their lived experience.

When we reconnect with Sam and Frodo in the first chapter, **"The Taming of Sméagol,"** they have already been struggling for three days through the Emyn Muil. To compare timelines, Merry and Pippin have already escaped the orcs by this time, and Aragorn, Gimli, and Legolas have traversed most of Rohan on foot at this point. The inner journey is far more monotonous and far less of what one might consider an adventure.

Frodo feels a tremendous sense of urgency at time. No one is pressuring his journey forward, so he has had to take on the mantel of authority and responsibility. All he can think about is the time, how each day, hour, and even minute is precious. Part of why he feels this is because he has no sense for the distance or the route into Mordor. Frodo has no spatial scale for the quest, so all he can discern is time.

When the Ringwraith passes overhead both Frodo and Sam experience intense fear, but it is only Frodo who loses his sight for a time. The fear of the Nazgûl assaults the senses. It is significant that Frodo, and not Sam, loses his sight completely. Perhaps this is because he is more vulnerable to the power of the Nazgûl, both as the bearer of the Ring but also because he carries the knife wound from Weathertop. How telling that his sight begins to return with the view of the elven rope—there is a subtle magical sparring between the powers of good and evil here, but our attention is not drawn to it overmuch. This same kind of subtle magic appears later, when the rope comes untied as Sam evokes the name Galadriel.

Speaking of the elven rope—how long is thirty ells? Originally it was considered to be the length between the elbow and the end of the middle finger—but of course that is a variable length even among humans, let alone hobbits. In our world there is the French ell, the English ell, and the Flemish ell, but they are all somewhat different. The Viking ell, based on the elbow to middle finger length, is 18 inches. Knowing Tolkien's love of Icelandic mythology and language, one might assume this is the measurement he means. So 30 ells, if counted at 18 inches, would be 45 feet long. Of course, in the text it says Sam is measuring with his own arm, so it might simply be 30 of his own arm lengths from elbow to fingertip. However, Frodo equates 30 ells with

18 fathoms, and a fathom—which is measured from fingertip to fingertip on a full-grown man—is considered to be about six feet, or two yards. 18 fathoms is then 108 feet, so much longer than 45 feet. Nonetheless, that is a decent length of rope Sam is carrying in his pack, and it certainly saved the hobbits a dangerous climb down from the labyrinthine rocks of the Emyn Muil.

The storm that crosses over the Emyn Muil, and then on to the river Anduin and the city of Minas Tirith, is no ordinary storm. Thunder, lightning, and rain are described, yet the storm clouds appear to be a physical expression of Sauron's own dark thought. Again, the weather of the world and the struggles between the factions of Middle-earth mirror one another.

Frodo and Sam speak of the Moon, of how it is growing but will not be full for some days. Tolkien was extensively thorough in making sure the phases of the Moon aligned perfectly with the unfolding timeline of the story. Likewise, he was equally careful with describing the direction of the wind, and with making sure every move corresponded exactly with the coordinates of the map of Middle-earth. This is what he meant by the "inner consistency of reality" that allows a reader to give themselves up to secondary belief, or the enchantment of a secondary world.[2]

Finally, we get a closer glimpse of the creature Gollum, perhaps one of the most unique figures in all of storytelling. Notice that Gollum is referred to as "it" at first, an inhuman creature climbing headfirst down the cliff face.[3]

Yet Gollum becomes human in Frodo's eyes when Frodo suddenly recalls Gandalf's words: "Pity? It was Pity that stayed his hand. Pity, and Mercy, not to strike without need."[4] How interesting that this is the same argument Aragorn puts forward to Gimli, that they might not strike an old man simply out of fear—and that old man turned out to be Gandalf himself.[5] But Frodo, in this moment, recalls Gandalf's words: "For even the very wise cannot see all ends."[6] So, tying the threads of fate together, Frodo spares Gollum and binds him to himself with an oath—an oath sworn on the Ring. In the moment of the oath-swearing Sam sees a remarkable vision: Frodo has grown greater while Gollum has shrunk, and there is a shrouded power to Frodo.

---

2 Tolkien, *On Fairy-Stories*, 59.
3 Tolkien, *The Two Towers*, IV, i, 598.
4 Tolkien, *The Fellowship of the Ring*, I, ii, 58.
5 Tolkien, *The Two Towers*, III, v, 482.
6 Tolkien, *The Fellowship of the Ring*, I, ii, 58.

Perhaps this power comes from the Ring itself, but it may also come from Frodo's own will, which is growing due to his trials and suffering. Sam sees a kinship between Gollum and Frodo here, and recognizes that, remarkably, they can reach into each other's minds. In some ways Frodo and Gollum are the same person, or an expression of the same person making two separate choices—much in the same way that Gandalf and Saruman differ based on their choices. Sam's vision here is important, one to keep in mind for later in the tale.

We see immediately that Sméagol and Gollum are different persons, although contained in one body. Gollum says that Sméagol went away long ago, and he is lost because his precious was taken from him. This statement is noteworthy, since it seems that the person of Gollum developed in response to having the Ring for so long. But did Sméagol disappear with the Ring, or long before? In *The Hobbit*, Gollum is said to talk to himself, but he also talks to the Ring. In *The Hobbit* he refers to himself as "my precious," but in *The Lord of the Rings* "my precious," or "the Precious," definitely refers to the One Ring.[7]

As we begin chapter two, **"The Passage of the Marshes,"** we see how much of this inner part of the

---

7 Tolkien, *The Hobbit*, 83.

story, the true Quest, is taken up with thoughts of survival: food, shelter, exhaustion. The story moves at a paintakingly slow pace much of the time. Entertainment is not the story's primary purpose. Such narrative expression creates an experience of true heroism, which takes place in the mud and the desolation, far from praise or celebration. One can recall the heroism of those who died in the trenches of the Great War, in similar conditions of squalor and horror. Indeed, the Dead Marshes are one region of Middle-earth that Tolkien said took direct inspiration from his experiences in the war: the Battle of the Somme is memorialized in the stagnant eeriness of the marshes.

Gollum says that the Dead Marshes swallowed the graves of those who died in a great battle long ago. He is referring to the Last Alliance of Elves and Men, and the Battle of Dagorlad that took place before the Black Gates of Mordor. To give a context of the timeline, the Last Alliance was formed in year 3430 of the Second Age, and the Battle of Dagorlad took place four years later in 3434. Then the Siege of Barad-dûr lasted seven years, until Isildur cut the One Ring from Sauron's hand and he was defeated—bringing the Second Age to a close. So the Dead Marshes grew over the graves of those who fought in the Battle of Dagorlad throughout the course of the Third Age. Why the images of their bodies are preserved is unknown.

Frodo's experience of the Eye of Sauron seems to speak to it not being a physical eye, rather a psychic one: Sauron's terrible will, striving to see into the minds of others. In this chapter we also hear the remarkable conversation between Gollum and Sméagol which Sam overhears upon waking from sleep. Already here Gollum suggests that "She might help."[8] Who is she? We find out by the end of this book: "She" is Shelob, the massive spider, descendent of the primeval spider Ungoliant. At this point Gollum has not come to a conclusion, for Sméagol begs they not go that way—the pass of Cirith Ungol. Perhaps he is afraid for his own sake, but it seems that Sméagol is also genuinely concerned about Frodo.

As the three figures approach the Morannon, the Black Gate, the winged Nazgûl passes three times overhead. The last time it flies swiftly to the West. This is the same Nazgûl who flew over the camp of the Rohirrim after the parley with Saruman, the night that Pippin looked into the Palantír. Thus we learn that the first two chapters of Book IV encompass the entire time period described in Book III, from Boromir's death to Gandalf and Pippin's departure for Minas Tirith. The world moves at different paces in these two stories.

---

[8] Tolkien, *The Two Towers*, IV, ii, 619.

The opening of chapter three, **"The Black Gate Is Closed,"** gives us a description of the Land of Mordor. The map is worth studying to see how the two mountain ranges—the Ered Lithui in the north, and the Ephel Dúath on the west—come together and form the gateway to Mordor. The region itself is large, and the business of the hobbits is concerned mostly with the northwestern corner of Mordor, where the mountain of fire, Orodruin, stands over the plain.

Chapter four, **"Of Herbs and Stewed Rabbit,"** takes us into the forgotten land of Ithilien. As mentioned previously, the word *ithil* is Sindarin for Moon, which evolved from the Quenya, or High Elvish, word *isil*. These were some of the earliest words Tolkien invented, or discovered, in Elvish. In Ithilien—the land once named for the Moon, and for Isildur, Elendil's elder son—Frodo and Sam encounter for the first time the men of Gondor. The meeting seems to be one of those "chance meetings," as they say in Middle-earth. Of all the people they might meet on the road, they encounter Faramir—who we first heard mentioned by Boromir in Rivendell, when Boromir said that his brother had dreamed the riddling words: *"Seek for the Sword that was Broken. In Imladris it dwells."*[9] These words, by seeming

---

9 Tolkien, *The Fellowship of the Ring*, II, ii, 240.

chance, Frodo repeats back to Faramir—words that Faramir himself dreamed. That it was a dream that set in motion Boromir coming to Rivendell and participating in the Council of Elrond is in itself rather extraordinary, at least from a modern perspective. The Council was not called; it came together by synchronicity. Middle-earth is a world where dreams and their visionary messages matter. And that is the kind of person Faramir is too: one who takes the reality of dreams seriously.

In this first conflict of Men against Men that Sam and Frodo witness, we see the tensions between the different races of Men. Indeed, one cannot help but interpret some of the text here as carrying racist implications. The Men who have gone over to the Enemy are the Southrons and Easterlings, Men who are described as being fierce and having dark faces. Is this overt racism or unconscious racism on Tolkien's part? If one reads Tolkien's letters, it is clear that he does not consciously carry racist or white supremacist tendencies. But this is also a very problematic part of his story. I believe there is a conflation here, between archetypal language and concrete realities. Tolkien writes of a struggle between light and dark, between good and evil. In our language, "dark" and "night" are often used metaphorically to refer to evil, to difficulties, challenges, or suffering. For example, we speak of "dark times" or "a dark mood," and we understand the meaning of such phrases as "there is a dark storm cloud on the horizon," "we look forward to a brighter day," "we all see through a glass darkly," or "she felt light flood into her soul at that moment."[10] Are these valid metaphors to use? These are not metaphors used only within a white Euro-American context either. Metaphors of dark and light have been used all around the world by numerous cultures.

Archetypal darkness should not be conflated with archetypal evil, rather it is the task of the reader to recognize moments when the metaphors overlap.[11] An example in *The Fellowship of the Ring* of when they are not conflated, and indeed clearly distinguished, occurs when Tom Bombadil says: "He knew the dark under the stars when it was fearless—before the Dark Lord came from Outside."[12] The conflation of dark with evil and light with goodness is broken down many times in *The Lord of the Rings*—not least being Saruman the White, one of the most evil and treacherous figures in the story.

Nonetheless, the general use of darker-skinned Men as servants of Sauron is still highly problematic in my view. Yet when Sam sees one of the men of Harad

---

10 Richard Tarnas, personal communication, 22 October 2018.
11 Richard Tarnas, personal communication, 22 October 2018.
12 Tolkien, *The Fellowship of the Ring*, I, vii, 129.

die next to him, he immediately recognizes his humanity over his otherness: "He wondered what the man's name was and where he came from; and if he was really evil of heart, or what lies or threats had led him on the long march from his home; and if he would not really rather have stayed there in peace."[13] We must remember too how many Men of all races, and even Elves, were taken in by the lies of Sauron—and also the lies of Saruman. Sauron led to the downfall of the civilization of Númenor, because of his lies. I want to hold the difficult tensions and questions this part of the story evokes—not forgiving by any means its racist undertones, but also not throwing out the whole story because of them either. Tolkien saw *The Lord of the Rings* as a translation of *The Red Book of Westmarch*. This seems to leave open an invitation for new translations: new ways of reading this story so the core symbolic narrative might shine through, despite the flawed vessel carrying its essence.

In the fifth chapter, **"The Window on the West,"** we see Faramir weighing as best he can what to do with Frodo and Sam. While we as readers know Frodo's full tale and Quest, Faramir does not—not yet. The way Faramir entered into this story is most interesting. In a letter to his son Christopher, dated May 6, 1944, Tolkien

---

13 Tolkien, *The Two Towers*, IV, iv, 646.

wrote: "A new character has come on the scene (I am sure I did not invent him, I did not even want him, though I like him, but there he came walking into the woods of Ithilien): Faramir, the brother of Boromir."[14] Notice the way Tolkien speaks of Faramir's agency. He was not made up, or invented, but so clearly has his own life and being within the imaginal world.

What a noble figure Faramir is. Speaking of Isildur's Bane, he says: "I would not take this thing, if it lay by the highway. Not were Minas Tirith falling in ruin and I alone could save her."[15] He speaks of his love of the city, the city of the Men of Númenor, wishing to see it once more as the flowering queen of cities, Minas Anor.

An interesting aside: Faramir and Sam are the same age—born the same year. They are both 36 years old at this moment in the story. They have led very different lives, but have walked the Earth for the same number of years of the Sun.

When Faramir and his men return to the cave behind the waterfall, the window on the west, they share an evening meal. Before the meal begins, all the men face westward for a moment of silence. Faramir explains: "So we always do, we look towards Númenor that was,

---

14 Tolkien, *Letters*, 79.
15 Tolkien, *The Two Towers*, IV, v, 656.

and beyond to Elvenhome that is, and to that which is beyond Elvenhome and will ever be."[16] Númenor is the land of his ancestry, and it drowned during the Second Age when the world was bent from a flat Earth into a planetary globe. Elvenhome refers to the island of Tol Eressëa, which stands within sight of the light of the Blessed Realm. And that which is beyond Elvenhome is the Blessed Realm itself: Aman, with its city of the gods, Valinor.

The isle of Númenor was destroyed because the Númenoreans, as Faramir says, longed for eternal life, and they tried to assault the Blessed Land and take it by force. Yet they could not have succeeded in wresting immortality from the Valar, because it was not in their human nature to live forever. The gift of Ilúvatar was the gift of death, the gift to leave the circles of the world. But influenced by Sauron's lies the Númenoreans thought the Valar were keeping immortality from them. Thus, when the last king of Númenor set foot on the blessed shoreline of Aman, the Valar begged of Ilúvatar for help, and Ilúvatar intervened in the world, bending the seas so that all of Númenor drowned and the great fleet of the king was pulled into the open abyss. Ilúvatar removed both Elvenhome and the Blessed Realm

---

16 Tolkien, *The Two Towers*, IV, v, 661.

from the circles of the world. Now if one sails westward they will no longer reach the immortal lands, they will instead circumnavigate the globe. But there is one path left: the Straight Road, an invisible path one could sail westward if granted permission to pass that way. When the Elves leave Middle-earth forever, they are sailing the Straight Road. Tolkien wrote of the Straight Road, and the downfall of Númenor, not only in the legendarium of Middle-earth, but even in his more contemporary tales *The Lost Road* and *The Notion Club Papers* that I discussed previously. The Straight Road appeared in Tolkien's imagination quite early in his writing of the mythology. I have even wondered if his *Ishness* drawing called *End of the World*, which shows a man stepping straight off a cliff above the sea, depicts a man stepping onto the Straight Road. Would he keep walking, traveling straight westward until he reached the Undying Lands, the Realm of Faërie? In Tolkien's earliest telling of the mythology, in *The Book of Lost Tales*, Tolkien wrote of a road called Olórë Mallë, the Path of Dreams. It was a path by which human children might travel in sleep to Valinor, to the Blessed Realm. Tolkien soon abandoned this idea, but I think it still remains in the image of the Straight Road. We can come to Faërie by way of our dreams. The first word of that name, Olórë Mallë, has the same root word, *olor*, as Gandalf's original

Maia name before he came to Middle-earth as the Grey Pilgrim. His name was Olórin. The root of that name, *olor*, means "dream." Furthermore, *olor* is derived from Quenya *olo-s* which means "vision, phantasy."[17] The name Olórin refers to visionary dreams.

The following three chapters—"The Forbidden Pool," "The Journey to the Crossroads," and "The Stairs of Cirith Ungol"—show the development and struggle within Gollum between his two selves: being tested in his trust, almost reaching redemption, and then failing to change and betraying his companions. As we try to fathom the complex figure of Gollum, we can recognize that he becomes the person he is in direct response to the actions of Faramir and the two hobbits. Those with whom we are in relationship intimately shape who we are.

In **"The Forbidden Pool,"** Frodo saves Gollum's life in the only way he can, and yet he knows his actions will seem like betrayal to the treacherous Gollum. We often suspect others of our own actions, projecting who we are onto those around us. Gollum is a severely traumatized creature, and Faramir's questioning pushes Gollum to his edge. He seeks refuge in his connection to Frodo, but it is a bond that is already weak, and

---

17 Verlyn Flieger, *A Question of Time: J. R. R. Tolkien's Road to Faërie* (Kent, OH: The Kent State UP, 1997), 166.

weakening further. Faramir can read Gollum well, and intuits his treachery despite any promises to the contrary. He says his heart warns him. Intuition is a knowing of the heart. The name of the pass, Cirith Ungol, is for Faramir filled with dread. He does not know what terror dwells in the passes above Minas Morgul, but the answer to that lies in the name itself, as is the case with all the names in Tolkien's stories. Ungol refers to Ungoliant, who was a primeval spider as old as the world itself. The first Dark Lord Morgoth formed an evil alliance with her, and together they destroyed the Two Trees of Valinor—the spider Ungoliant hungers after light, and she poisoned and sucked the Two Trees dry of their light. The world was cast into darkness, and it was only after mourning and coaxing forth by Yavanna, the Vala who sang the Two Trees into being, that they gave their final fruit and flower that would become the Sun and the Moon. This is the tale that the name Cirith Ungol recalls with dread and terror.

Chapter seven, "**Journey to the Crossroads**," takes place during the day without dawn. The Dawnless Day is a marker for the many divergent timelines of this story. We will hear it described several more times in *The Return of the King*.

The final scene of this chapter unveils the vision of the statue of the king with a crown again, the trailing silver and gold flowers around his brow lit by the setting sunlight. We are given but a glimpse, as Tolkien writes. Take note of each time Tolkien uses the word "glimpse." It is a favorite word of his. He uses it in his short stories and his essays, as when he says that fantasy is "the making or glimpsing of Other-worlds."[18] His many uses of the word "glimpse," which comes from the Middle English word meaning "to shine faintly," seem to indicate that something more is shining through mundane reality: the beyond, the ineffable, the divine pierces through the veils for just a moment to remind us that there is hope beyond our darkest days.

The eighth chapter, **"The Stairs of Cirith Ungol,"** contains one of the most profound moments of self-awareness in the entire book: when Sam begins speaking about the tales he loved to listen to, adventures as he used to call them. Frodo and Sam realize they too are in a story, and not only that but they are a part of a much longer story, stretching back to the First Age—a story of the light that is in Frodo's starglass from Galadriel, which is the light of Eärendil, the Silmaril rescued by Lúthien and Beren. That Silmaril contains the blended light of the Two Trees of Valinor, captured in a crystalline casing by the greatest of all

---

18 Tolkien, *On Fairy-Stories*, 55.

craftsmen, Fëanor. As Sam says: "Don't the great tales never end?"[19] And then he reaches perhaps the most self-referential, meta moment in the story, a moment that as the scholar Verlyn Flieger says is both postmodern and medieval.[20] Sam muses:

> Still, I wonder if we shall ever be put into songs or tales. We're in one, of course; but I mean: put into words, you know, told by the fireside, or read out of a great big book with red and black letters, years and years afterwards. And people will say: "Let's hear about Frodo and the Ring!"[21]

For indeed this tale is recorded in a great big book with red and black letters—*The Red Book of Westmarch*. These passages are worth reading again, to deepen into what the hobbits are really saying. Frodo says: "Why Sam, to hear you somehow makes me as merry as if the story was already written."[22] For indeed it is already written. We hold that book in our hands. We are in two places at once, inside and outside the tale as the

---

19 Tolkien, *The Two Towers*, IV, viii, 697.
20 Verlyn Flieger, "A Post-Modern Medievalist," in *Green Suns and Faërie: Essays on J. R. R. Tolkien*, 259.
21 Tolkien, *The Two Towers*, IV, viii, 697.
22 Tolkien, *The Two Towers*, IV, viii, 697.

tale refers to itself. The world bends in on itself in that moment, and the outer world of common day and the inner world of the imaginal realm become one.

The final scene in this exquisite chapter is a deeply poignant one. Gollum returns, and as we know from how the story unfolds, he has already betrayed the two hobbits to the spider Shelob. The hobbits are asleep, and as Gollum looks at Frodo he, for a moment, fully returns to being Sméagol. The gleam fades from his eyes and he looks like an old, tired hobbit. He is a truly tragic figure. And this moment of repentance could have saved everything—he might not have betrayed the two hobbits as he intended. He might have been able to become whole once more, and no longer divided. But when Sam awakens he is immediately suspicious, and it is that suspicion which pushes Sméagol away forever. As Tolkien writes: "The fleeting moment had passed, beyond recall."[23] The betrayal of Gollum is now inevitable.

The final two chapters, *"Shelob's Lair"* and "The Choices of Master Samwise," contain the moment of true initiation for both hobbits, particularly for Sam. The ordeal is horrifying, but the strength of Sam's courage finally shines forth. Here at last we see the great and terrible ancient power of night: the spider Shelob. The

---

23 Tolkien, *The Two Towers*, IV, viii, 699.

giant spider as a symbol of night was part of Tolkien's legendarium from the earliest beginnings. In a brief note jotted down in the winter of 1914 that sketches out the stages of Eärendil's sea voyage, Tolkien wrote: "The home of Night. The Spider. He escapes from the meshes of Night with a few comrades."[24] The great spider is one of the earliest and most enduring images in Tolkien's legendarium, first emerging in this note at the time of *The Book of Ishness*, and reappearing as the "primeval spirit Móru" who takes "the guise of an unlovely spider" in *The Book of Lost Tales*.[25] No one knows her origin, but it is thought that "she has always been."[26] This spider is also named Ungwë Lianti, and is later called Ungoliant. She is the destroyer of the Two Trees of Valinor. The giant spiders reemerge in *The Hobbit*, ensnaring Bilbo and the thirteen dwarves in their webs woven in the darkness of Mirkwood.[27] And finally, the image of the spider returns once more in the form of Shelob.

Frodo intuitively pulls out the star-glass of Galadriel when they enter the pitch darkness of the tunnel,

---

24 Tolkien, "The Tale of Eärendel," 261.

25 J.R.R. Tolkien, "The Theft of Melko," in *The History of Middle-Earth: The Book of Lost Tales, Part I*, vol. 1, ed. Christopher Tolkien, (New York: Houghton Mifflin, 2010), 151–52.

26 Tolkien, "The Theft of Melko," 152.

27 Tolkien, *The Hobbit*, 166–76

and we see here an extraordinary recapitulation of the primal struggle between darkness and light from the First Age of the world. Frodo faces the ancient spider Shelob, the last child of Ungoliant, the spider who destroyed the Two Trees. Frodo holds aloft the star-glass that contains the light from Eärendil's Silmaril, the last remnant of the blended light of the Two Trees, and the starry light prevails. Here, on the borders of hell, two seemingly insignificant hobbits play out once more the primal conflict that began when time was still young.

Frodo calls out a prayer in Elvish to Eärendil: "*Aiya Eärendil Elenion Ancalima,*" which means "Hail Eärendil, brightest of stars."[28] This line echoes the original Anglo-Saxon line Tolkien first read back in 1913 that initiated the writing of his whole mythology: Éalá Éarendel engla beorhtast, "Hail Éarendel, brightest of angels."[29] The light of Eärendil and the darkness of the great spider were each there from the beginning, entering Tolkien's imagination in 1913 and 1914. This is the heart of all the stories of Middle-earth.

In the last chapter of Book IV, "**The Choices of Master Samwise,**" Sam comes fully into his own. Sam's love for Frodo drives his actions, and he faces a great-

---

28 Tolkien, *The Two Towers*, IV, ix, 704.
29 Carpenter, *Tolkien: A Biography*, 72.

er fear than perhaps all the members of the Fellowship when he fights against Shelob. He uses her own will and weight against herself. And by holding aloft the star-glass, Sam connects to a power beyond him—he speaks spontaneously in strange tongues, crying a prayer to Elbereth in a language he does not know, Sindarin. The prayer echoes the song sung months before in Rivendell.

> *A Elbereth Gilthoniel*
> O Star-Queen, Star-Kindler
>
> *o menel palan-díriel*
> from firmament afar gazing
> *le nallon si di'nguruthos!*
> to thee I cry beneath death-horror!
>
> *A tiro nin, Fanuilos!*
> O watch over me, Fanuilos![30]

This translation also comes from Ruth Noel, from her book *The Languages of Tolkien's Middle-earth*. Shelob is defeated, wounded but not destroyed, and Sam now sees his worst fear play out: Frodo, seemingly dead. Sam's response is heartbreaking: "Don't leave me here

---

30 Tolkien, *The Two Towers*, IV, x, 712; Noel, *The Languages of Tolkien's Middle-Earth*, 40.

alone! It's your Sam calling. Don't go where I can't follow!"[31] He remembers his vision from the Mirror of Galadriel, the vision that foretold this moment.[32] The true initiation though, is not Sam facing the spider, it is his coming to the realization that he must see the task through to the end, to bring the Ring to the fire and destroy it. He realizes he has been chosen against his desires, just as Frodo was. And Samwise is able to awaken to his wisdom and make the right choices, choices that save everything. Sam could not have known Frodo was only poisoned, not dead, without the orcs saying so. And he could not have evaded them or even heard clearly what they said without taking the Ring and putting it on. But wearing the Ring was also the greatest risk he could take. He is indeed walking upon a knife edge, and each choice is perilous. He chooses the Quest first, and knows he must go on, and this is right. But when he learns Frodo is still alive, he makes the choice to try to save him, and this too is right. He begins his ownership of the Ring by thinking of another, by being in a place of love. Just as Bilbo began his ownership of the Ring with pity, by sparing Gollum, Sam begins his with love and thus too is given some protection from its evil effects.

---

31 Tolkien, *The Two Towers*, IV, x, 712.
32 Tolkien, *The Fellowship of the Ring*, II, vii, 353.

Interlude

The Myth of Creation and the Source of Evil

J.R.R. TOLKIEN FIRST WROTE his creation myth *The Music of the Ainur* in 1919 and included it in *The Book of Lost Tales*. He later renamed it the *Ainulindalë*, and this cosmogony opens *The Silmarillion*. The creation myth begins with the supreme deity, Ilúvatar, who is also named Eru. Emanated from Eru, the One, are the multiplicity of Ainur. Ilúvatar propounds the Ainur to bring forth a great music that is of his devising, and yet is given voice through each of the Ainur. Ilúvatar invites each of the Ainur to exercise their minds and powers in adorning the theme to their own thoughts and devising. The Ainur are the first sub-creators, to use Tolkien's own term. They are creators through whom the creativity of God is channeled and given unique form.

As the Music of the Ainur progresses, and overflows and creates echoes upon echoes into far and empty regions, desire comes into the heart of Melko—or Melkor, as Tolkien would later alter his name. Melko wishes "to interweave matters of his own vain imagining that were not fitting to that great theme of Ilúvatar."[1] Each of the Ainur had been given permission to adorn the theme of the music with their own thoughts, but when Melko chooses to do so, something seemingly unexpected occurs. When his "devisings and imaginings" are woven into the music, "straightway harshness and discordancy rose about him."[2] Why are Melko's themes apparently at odds with Ilúvatar's? Why is there a clash of opposites? In the original telling of *The Music of the Ainur* in *The Book of Lost Tales*, the reason given is that "those thoughts of his came from the outer blackness whither Ilúvatar had not yet turned the light of his face; and because his secret thoughts had no kinship with the beauty of Ilúvatar's design its harmonies were broken and destroyed."[3] Melko had wandered "alone into the dark places and the voids seeking the Secret Fire," because he desired to bring forth life and being in the same manner that Ilúvatar did.[4] Yet Melko found that the Secret Fire was not in the void, and he brought back its darkness into the music instead.

[1] Tolkien, "The Music of the Ainur," in *The History of Middle-Earth: The Book of Lost Tales, Part I*, vol. 1, ed. Christopher Tolkien, (New York: Houghton Mifflin Company, 2010), 53.
[2] Tolkien, "The Music of the Ainur," 54.
[3] Tolkien, "The Music of the Ainur," 54.
[4] Tolkien, "The Music of the Ainur," 53.

Interlude: The Myth of Creation and the Source of Evil   145

What is this darkness? What is the void? If one returns to the beginning of *The Music of the Ainur*, it begins with the words "Ilúvatar dwelt alone."[5] However, as the Gnostic scholar Lance Owens has observed, there is also an unseen outer darkness behind Ilúvatar, where he has not turned the light of his face. Owens suggests that perhaps Ilúvatar is not actually alone. Behind Ilúvatar is a shadow, of which he is unaware and unconscious.[6] When Melko wanders in the darkness of the void, he forms of that experience his own independent thoughts, and weaves these into the music, creating discord and ill harmony. Melko has suffused the light with darkness, bringing the two natures of light and dark together. Before the music begins there is a "potential duality" between the light of Ilúvatar and the darkness of the void.[7] Because they are static and inactive, they could be considered a unity.

As the clash and disharmony in the music progresses in the *Ainulindalë*, Ilúvatar raises his left hand with a smile and introduces a new theme. The new theme grows in "power and sweetness"; and yet against it

---

5   Tolkien, "The Music of the Ainur," 52.
6   Owens, personal communication, 29 October 2015.
7   Owens, personal communication, 29 October 2015.

Melko's discord rages all the more violently.[8] Now weeping, Ilúvatar raises his right hand and a third theme is introduced, that is unlike any of the prior themes:

> For it seemed at first soft and sweet, a mere rippling of gentle sounds in delicate melodies; but it could not be quenched, and it took to itself power and profundity. And it seemed at last that there were two musics progressing at one time before the seat of Ilúvatar, and they were utterly at variance. The one was deep and wide and beautiful, but slow and blended with immeasurable sorrow, from which its beauty chiefly came. The other had now achieved a unity of its own; but it was loud, and vain, and endlessly repeated . . . In the midst of this strife . . . Ilúvatar arose a third time, and his face was terrible to behold. Then he raised up both his hands, and in one chord, deeper than the Abyss, higher than the Firmament, piercing as the light of the eye of Ilúvatar, the Music ceased.[9]

When the music comes to its great end, Ilúvatar shows to the Ainur a vision of the world that is to be, the world

---

8   Tolkien, "The Music of the Ainur," 54.
9   J.R.R. Tolkien, *The Silmarillion*, ed. Christopher Tolkien, (New York: Houghton Mifflin, 2001), 16–17.

whose design was contained within the music. As he does so, Ilúvatar speaks to Melko, saying: "Thou Melko shalt see that no theme can be played save it come in the end of Ilúvatar's self, nor can any alter the music in Ilúvatar's despite."[10] Ilúvatar names the terrors and sorrows, cruelties and violences that Melko has introduced into the music, and therefore into the world. And yet, Ilúvatar states that these evils come "through him and not by him."[11] Melko, too, is but a sub-creator; Ilúvatar takes full responsibility not only for the good of the world, but the evil. As Ilúvatar states, the suffering caused by that evil will make "Life more worth the living, and the World so much the more wonderful and marvellous, that of all the deeds of Ilúvatar it shall be called his mightiest and his loveliest."[12]

The greatest difference between the early 1919 telling of *The Music of the Ainur* and Tolkien's later rendition of the *Ainulindalë* included in *The Silmarillion*, pertains to the source of Melko's discord. Both versions tell of his wandering in the void, but only in the early version is the void described as "the outer blackness whither Ilúvatar had not yet turned the light of

[10] Tolkien, "The Music of the Ainur," 55.
[11] Tolkien, "The Music of the Ainur," 55.
[12] Tolkien, "The Music of the Ainur," 55.

his face."[13] In the later version, it is simply Melko's perception that "Ilúvatar took no thought for the Void, and he was impatient of its emptiness."[14] Likewise, in the first version Melko's musical themes have "no kinship with the beauty of Ilúvatar's design," whereas in the later revision the thoughts of Melkor (whose name has been slightly altered) differ from those of the Ainur, not from Ilúvatar himself.[15] The potential dualism between light and dark, and between good and evil, is more pronounced in the first version of Tolkien's *Music of the Ainur*, whereas some of those tensions have been made less stark in the later revision. But in both versions we learn how evil was introduced into the very structure of the world.

Perhaps one of the reasons Tolkien made these subtle editorial changes was to bring his creation myth into greater accord with his devotion to Catholic dogma. Nonetheless, the later telling of the *Ainulindalë* still expresses many qualities of Gnosticism and Manichaeism.[16] As the scholar Carol Fry relates: "Tolkien's

---

13 Tolkien, "The Music of the Ainur," 54.

14 Tolkien, *The Silmarillion*, 16.

15 Tolkien, "The Music of the Ainur," 54; Tolkien, *The Silmarillion*, 16.

16 Lance S. Owens, "Tolkien, Jung, and the Imagination" (Interview with Miguel Conner. *AeonBytes Gnostic Radio*, April 2011); Carrol Fry, "'Two Musics about the Throne of Ilúvatar,' Gnostic and

portrayal of Ilúvatar, also far beyond the material world, resembles the Unknown God. Sometimes called the Monad, the Gnostic Unknown God created the Pleroma and like Ilúvatar 'emanated' spiritual beings the Gnostics called Aeons."[17] Furthermore, Fry notes some resemblance between the Gnostic Demiurge—the image of whom was informed in part by the Demiurge of Plato's *Timaeus*—and the fallen Melkor, who desires to possess the world of Arda for himself, and to make his own created beings: "This shall be my own kingdom and I name it unto myself," Melkor declares.[18] Of course, there is also a clear corollary between Melkor and the fallen Lucifer of the Christian tradition. Understanding the origin myth that stands behind the legendarium of Middle-earth can shed new light upon the workings of evil as they appear in *The Lord of the Rings*, offering a background and a pretext for how the dialectic between evil and good unfolds in the narrative.

Manichaean Dualism in *The Silmarillion*," *Tolkien Studies* 12 (2015): 82; Joscelyn Godwin, "Tolkien and the Primordial Tradition" (Paper given at the Second International Conference on the Fantastic in the Arts, at Florida Atlantic University, 18–21 March 1981), 2.

17 Fry, "Two Musics about the Throne of Ilúvatar," 83.

18 Tolkien, *The Silmarillion*, 21; Fry, "Two Musics about the Throne of Ilúvatar," 84.

Cirith Ungol

5

The Return of the King – *Book V*
In the Land of Gondor

THE MOVEMENT FROM INNER QUEST to outer shifts again between the end of *The Two Towers* and *The Return of the King*. Tolkien's preferred title for the third volume of *The Lord of the Rings* was actually *The War of the Ring*, and we can see why in Book V. We come to the front lines of the war against Sauron, and the last defense of the Free Peoples of Middle-earth.

In the first chapter, "**Minas Tirith**," we reconnect with Pippin and Gandalf, riding Shadowfax faster than the wind across the realm of Gondor. Gandalf refers to the land of Anórien through which they are passing. Why is it called Anórien? The name is the complement to Ithilien, the land into which Frodo, Sam, and Gollum just entered at this time. The roots of these names, Anórien and Ithilien, are the Elvish words for Sun and Moon, *Anór* and *Ithil*. Just to reiterate, the names of the towers that oversaw these lands were Minas Anor and Minas Ithil. We have already seen the ruin that Minas

Ithil has become through Frodo's eyes: the ghastly haunted abode of the Nazgûl, Minas Morgul, the Tower of Dark Sorcery. Now in this first chapter of *The Return of the King* we come to what Minas Anor has become: Minas Tirith, the Tower of Guard. And indeed, that is exactly what this magnificent city is: the final fortification and defense against Sauron, a bulwark at the base of Mount Mindolluin.

The seven circles and gates of the city echo a city of the First Age, the hidden city of Gondolin that was central to the first tale Tolkien ever wrote of Middle-earth: *The Fall of Gondolin*. That ancient city was hidden within a ring of mountains, and was guarded by seven gates just as Minas Tirith is. Also, Gondolin shares a root word with the name Gondor: *gond* meaning "stone." So Gondor translates as "stone-land." The second syllable, *dor*, is in the names of other lands such as Mordor and Eriador in the north. Minas Tirith has a white tower called the Tower of Ecthelion. This tower was named after the steward Ecthelion who rebuilt it three centuries before the War of the Ring. This is a different Ecthelion than the father of Denethor. However, the original bearer of the name Ecthelion was an elf who lived in the ancient Elvish city Gondolin. Ecthelion fought one-on-one with the Balrog Gothmog during the sack of Gondolin, and both Ecthelion and Gothmog fell into the Fountain of the King and drowned. There are many echoes in the history and nomenclature between Minas Tirith and Gondolin.

As Pippin and Gandalf enter the citadel, we learn that nothing is known in Minas Tirith of Aragorn, the long-surviving heir of Isildur. Aragorn has lived his long life in secret, and although he has fought in the wars of Gondor and Rohan, he has not revealed his identity to anyone. His time has not been ripe, and that secrecy has kept him safe—especially from Sauron, who fears the Sword of Elendil that cut the Ring from his hand. Gandalf foreshadows the manner of Aragorn's arrival when he says: "if he comes, it is likely to be in some way that no one expects."[1] And indeed, that is the case, as we see in the coming chapters.

The history of Númenor is what shapes the culture of Gondor. The statues inside the citadel, Pippin notices, resemble the Argonath, the great statues of Isildur and Anárion standing over the Great River. Likewise, Denethor resembles Aragorn, for the blood of Númenor is in them both.

Pippin swears fealty to Denethor, and to Gondor, just as in the following chapter Meriadoc swears his

---

[1] J. R. R. Tolkien, *The Lord of the Rings: The Return of the King* (New York: Houghton Mifflin, 2014), V, i, 737.

service to Théoden and to Rohan. Once separated, the two hobbits still mirror or parallel each other in their stories. And yet Merry feels a love for Théoden that is different than the fear but also pride Pippin feels in response to Denethor. The two hobbits need to be separated so they can mature and develop—so they can individuate and fulfill their unique roles in this narrative.

In Pippin's conversations in Gondor, we learn that his accent sounds strange. While this is something we cannot hear when simply reading the books, it indicates how very far apart the Shire in Eriador in the north is from Gondor in the south. And Tolkien, ever keen to make notice of language, dialect, and accent, is careful to remark on the hobbit's accent several times.

Beregond gives Pippin the lay of the land as it can be seen from the walls of Minas Tirith, and we can see the ruins of Osgiliath in the distance spanning the Great River. Beregond speaks of the villages and lands to the south: Tumladen, Lossarnach, Lebennin. It is worth familiarizing oneself with the map once more, looking now to the far south, to the lands between Minas Tirith and the Bay of Belfalas. These are the same lands Aragorn and the Grey Company traverse when they pass through with the Host of the Dead. These are the lands from which the various companies come to Minas Tirith that Pippin and the young Bergil watch entering the city at the end of the first chapter. We gain a brief glimpse into the cultures of these different men, their stories embedded in the colors and emblems on their many banners as they march into the city, the many peoples who come to add their numbers to those who defend Minas Tirith and guard Middle-earth.

"The board is set, and the pieces are moving," Gandalf says.[2] And that is how Book V is structured, moving from chess piece to chess piece. The day without dawn, once again, acts as an anchor in time so we can see how the many divergent timelines of the story align with each other.

The second chapter, **"The Passing of the Grey Company,"** takes us back to the four members of the Fellowship who were left in Rohan: Aragorn, Merry, Gimli, and Legolas. Here we meet more of the Dúnedain, Aragorn's kinsmen from the north. Within two chapters we meet two of the kindreds of Númenor, from the south and the north. How different, in some ways, the men of Gondor are from the Rangers. They have been shaped by their homes and ecological habitats, adapted to city and stone in the south, and to the forest and the wild in the north. Yet they share a common ancestry. We learn directly from Halbarad how the

---

2   Tolkien, *The Return of the King*, V, i, 743.

Rangers have guarded the Shire, allowing the hobbits the peace in which they have quietly tilled their lands for so many generations. It is as though, unconsciously, the Dúnedain guarded the hobbits' innocence so that someday a few humble hobbits might emerge to change the fortunes of all in Middle-earth.

After looking in the Palantír, Aragorn makes the decision to follow the Paths of the Dead. He does so because Elrond has sent a message to him through the Dúnedain, reminding him of the words of Malbeth the Seer, a prophesy spoken hundreds of years prior:

> *Over the land there lies a long shadow,*
> *westward reaching wings of darkness.*
> *The Tower trembles; to the tombs of kings*
> *doom approaches. The Dead awaken;*
> *for the hour is come for the oathbreakers:*
> *at the Stone of Erech they shall stand again*
> *and hear there a horn in the hills ringing.*
> *Whose shall the horn be? Who shall call them*
> *from the grey twilight, the forgotten people?*
> *The heir of him to whom the oath they swore.*
> *From the North shall he come, need shall drive him:*
> *he shall pass the Door to the Paths of the Dead.*[3]

---

3 Tolkien, *The Return of the King*, V, ii, 764.

The Tower that trembles may be Minas Tirith, but it may also be Sauron's tower of Barad-Dûr. The line "to the tombs of kings doom approaches," foreshadows the scene with Denethor and Faramir in Rath Dínen, in the chapter "The Pyre of Denethor."

In the confrontation between Éowyn and Aragorn before Aragorn departs from Dunharrow, we learn how greatly Éowyn has struggled and suffered within the restrictive role of her life as a woman. She can fight as a warrior and does not fear pain or death, and yet she has had to follow the duties expected of her. She is bitter. She sees her gendered role to be confining and without honor. To add further injury to this hurt, Aragorn cryptically reveals where his own heart dwells—in Rivendell, with Arwen. At the end of this conversation, Éowyn comes as close as she can to admitting her love for Aragorn, when she says of his companions that they will not be parted from him because they love him. She has made clear that it is also her desire to accompany him on his dark road, a desire which he has reminded her she cannot follow because of her duty to her own people.

The Paths of the Dead carry a fear unlike any other underground journey in *The Lord of the Rings*. The Dark Door brings to mind Tolkien's early 1912 drawing from *The Book of Ishness* that he titled *Before*, showing a monolithic doorway leading into darkness. Indeed, this dark doorway appears again and again in Tolkien's later writings and artwork: the imposing doorway reappears in drawings of the underground Elvish dwelling Nargothrond from the First Age,[4] and in *The Hobbit* in several images of the entryway to the Elvenking's underground halls.[5] A doorway of that same shape is also on the jacket cover Tolkien painted for *The Hobbit*.[6] Furthermore, that same dark doorway filled with red light appears in a pencil and ink illustration of the tower of Barad-dûr in Mordor.[7] One has the distinct impression that Tolkien had seen this dark doorway in dream, or vision, and that the image remained with him for many years.

Tolkien mentions a vision of this Door in his unfinished story *The Notion Club Papers*, and it seems highly likely that he is referring to the door in *Before* that he drew in 1912. The character Michael Ramer speaks of yet "another symbol" he has seen in a dream sequence. Ramer says: "the Great Door, shaped like a Greek π with sloping sides.... Then the Door opens—but no! I have no words for that Fear."[8] The encounter with this dark

---

4 Hammond and Scull, *Artist & Illustrator*, 60.
5 Hammond and Scull, *Artist & Illustrator*, 127–28.
6 Hammond and Scull, *Artist & Illustrator*, 151.
7 Hammond and Scull, *Artist & Illustrator*, 145.
8 Tolkien, "The Notion Club Papers," 206.

doorway seems always to be accompanied by a feeling of foreboding and fear: those attendant feelings are carried into Tolkien's many descriptions of the door throughout his writings. The fear is not simply of the unknown, but of what awaits in the darkness, which may have an evil or sinister purpose and will.

Significant thresholds at the entrance to underground realms appear with such frequency in all of Tolkien's stories that they punctuate the narratives with a deep, ominous rhythm. We have the doorway into Moria, the dark tunnel entrance to Torech Ungol—Shelob's Lair that Frodo and Sam enter—and now, the doorway to the Paths of the Dead, accompanied by a greater fear than any of the Grey Company has ever known before. On the journey through the Paths of the Dead, Aragorn at last meets his true initiation and comes into his own. This is the moment for which he has been waiting, for so many years. He shows the power of his will and the lineage he wields. There is a reason it was not until Aragorn, son of Arathorn, that the heir of kings could return to his throne. The lineage culminates in Aragorn, and through his command, even of the Dead, we see who he truly is.

We circle back yet again in chapter three, "**The Muster of Rohan,**" to more of the chess pieces moving across the board of this story. Merry is with Théoden and the people of Rohan as they arrive in Dunharrow. Here we learn that once more the plan has been changed, and that the muster of Rohan will not happen in the open fields by Edoras—where we first met King Théoden—but in the secret hideaway in the mountains at Dunharrow. Théoden only returns home briefly before he rides once more to war. It is perhaps odd that when Merry meets Dernhelm he says he does not know the rider's name. At this point it seems that Éowyn was not planning to conceal her identity from him, but since Merry says he does not know her name she just says: "Then call me Dernhelm."[9]

Once more the story pivots back to Minas Tirith in the fourth chapter, **"The Siege of Gondor."** For the first time we truly witness Gandalf's increased power, as he rides Shadowfax against five of the Nazgûl in the air. This is always Tolkien's way when showing supernatural power—it is hidden for most of the time, and even when revealed it is subtle or simply displayed. At the sight of white light radiating seemingly from Gandalf's hand, the Nazgûl retreat. But we can also see Gandalf's fear and weakness in this same chapter, as he trembles with anxiety while Faramir reports to Denethor of his chance meeting with Frodo and Sam

---

9 Tolkien, *The Return of the King*, V, iii, 787.

in Ithilien. When Denethor hears Faramir's story he is able to put together far more than he reveals. Denethor knows much more than he should for one who does not travel abroad. Indeed, he often hints as much, almost as though he wants the source of his knowledge to be discovered. Which, of course, we finally discover when at last he falls into utter despair and seeks to burn himself and Faramir in the chapter "The Pyre of Denethor." His source is one of the Palantíri, one of the seeing stones of Gondor. After Faramir's wounded body is first brought back to the city, Denethor retreats into a secret room in the Tower of Ecthelion, and a light flickers from the window. This is the light from the Palantír, as Denethor has gazed into it once more and returned without hope. He believes that Sauron has found the Ring when he says: "The fool's hope has failed. . . . he sees our very thoughts, and all we do is ruinous."[10] Sauron has mastered Denethor through the stone, able to show him what he will. Denethor's own arrogance has blinded him to the way the Dark Lord has toyed with him. The role Pippin plays in relation to Denethor stands out. Even though he was moved to swear fealty to him, when Faramir's life is on the line he recognizes Denethor's madness and not only plans quickly but also disobeys

---

10 Tolkien, *The Return of the King*, V, iv, 805.

him. This is the same Pippin who contrived his own escape from the Uruk-Hai, by thinking innovatively and understanding innately how others think.

Tolkien's descriptions of the siege itself speak as much of the organizational and strategic details of war as of the violence and fighting. We learn of the long labor upon the Pelennor, of orcs digging trenches. One can be sure that the image of trench warfare was in Tolkien's mind from his own experiences in the First World War. Perhaps one of the most chilling moments of the siege is when the heads of the fallen men of Gondor are catapulted over the walls. Reading this, I feel more sick than perhaps any other part of the War of the Ring. The Dark Lord wages war without pity, and without concern for his own hosts. It does not matter to him how many orcs or men he loses. They are dispensable. Sauron's will drives the orcs forward. They are enslaved to his will, rather than driven by loyalty. The focus of the assault on Minas Tirith is the Gate, which is hammered by Grond, a battering ram worthy of a name with a lineage. Grond is named after the first Dark Lord Morgoth's warhammer. The battering ram has the shape of a wolf, and is made in the likeness of the hellhound Carcharoth from *Beren and Lúthien*.

This chapter ends in an extraordinary crescendo. When the Gate breaks open the Lord of the Nazgûl enters—the first enemy ever to cross that threshold. All flee except Shadowfax and Gandalf. The Witch-King calls Gandalf an old fool, just as Denethor called him the Grey Fool not long before. Gandalf, who called nearly everyone a fool, is now the fool. Sending the Ring into Mordor turns out to have been merely a fool's hope.

In Tolkien's narrative, it appears that only the simple and humble can really counter evil in a way that is actually effective. Such simplicity humiliates evil, exposing its pride. Because, in that apparent moment of triumph for the Witch-King, a simple rooster crows. But the rooster heralds the dawn. And dawn was not supposed to come. The weather of the world once more prophesies the fortunes of those on the Earth. With the coming of dawn comes hope, and almost as if in response to the crow of the rooster, the horns of Rohan blow.

We circle back to Merry and the Riders of Rohan in the fifth chapter, **"The Ride of the Rohirrim."** We see two distinct forms of warfare between the previous chapter and this one: siege warfare in Gondor, and the cavalry warfare of the Rohirrim. The riders must travel light, with only enough food and water for the journey, alongside their weapons. It may be difficult to imagine what it must be like to ride for days on end, knowing that upon arrival you will need the strength to fight in battle.

In the Drúadan Forest we meet Ghân-buri-Ghân, leader of the Woses. As I mentioned previously, *wose* is an Anglo-Saxon word that Tolkien wove into the story, in connection with the Anglo-Saxon names and culture of the Rohirrim. The Woses, or the Drúedain, called themselves Drughu. They were the first human beings to migrate from the place where the Second Children of Ilúvatar—mortal humans—first awoke in the east of Middle-earth. Some came as far west as Beleriand in the First Age, where they encountered the Sindarin Elves, who called them the Drúedain, combining their own name for themselves—Drughu—with the Elvish word for "man," *adan*. The Drúedain mostly kept to themselves, a quiet, hidden people who may have had certain magical abilities and could sit in meditation for a long time. They made the statues of the Púkel-men that Merry saw in Dunharrow. The word "Púkel" comes from the Anglo-Saxon word for "goblin" or "troll." Sadly, the Rohirrim had a xenophobic loathing for the Woses, and would at times even hunt them in their forest. And yet, the Woses' fear of Sauron and hatred of the orcs led them to help the Rohirrim in their ride south to Gondor.

Once more a close examination of the map of Middle-earth provides valuable context. Trace the route the Rohirrim take, particularly along the Stonewain

Valley in the Drúadan Forest. Some editions of *The Lord of the Rings* have a close-up version of the map of Gondor, so one can identify the details in the topography, including the names of the beacons along the White Mountains between Minas Tirith and Edoras.

I keep bringing attention to the weather, in part because the figures in the narrative do as well. When Ghân-buri-Ghân departs, he says suddenly: "Wind is changing!"[11] This is our first hint of how the battle may go. Then the rider Wídfara also affirms that the weather is changing. The new wind from the south carries the scent of the sea, and the winds will sweep away Sauron's reeking airs and make way for the dawn. As in the Battle of the Hornburg, dawn brings hope and symbolizes victory over evil. And the scent of the sea carries with it the memory of Númenor, and of Elvenhome, and that which lies beyond Elvenhome. These symbols all point to who is sailing the winds of that sea-breeze: the last king of Númenor with his black standard, bearing the emblem of Elendil: *seven stars and seven stones and one white tree.*

Tolkien's language begins to shift at the end of this chapter into an ascended tone, a quality that carries over into the subsequent chapter, **"The Battle of the Pelennor Fields."** Tolkien uses exclamatory words,

---

11 Tolkien, *The Return of the King*, V, v, 817.

such as "Behold!" and "Lo!" mid-sentence. There is a gravitas to his language. This is a far cry from the hobbit narrative of the beginning of *The Fellowship of the Ring*.

This chapter opens onto one of the most powerful and moving scenes in the entirety of *The Lord of the Rings*. Théoden charges across the Pelennor in glory, but is then countered by the Captain of Sauron's hosts, the Lord of the Nazgûl. His many names are repeated throughout these chapters: once the Witch-king of Angmar far to the north, a sorcerer, and now a Ringwraith. As Gandalf iterated previously, a prophesy foretold that he would not be killed by the hand of man. The Witch-King's story receives greater attention in Appendix A. During the wars in the north that led to the fall of Arnor, the north-kingdom, the Witch-King was finally overthrown by a host from Gondor that joined forces with the elf Cirdan the Shipwright, and another host out of Rivendell led by Glorfindel. When Angmar was defeated, the Witch-King came forth once more alone, and charged straight for the captain of Gondor. While the captain was unafraid, his horse bolted, bearing the captain away. The Witch-King issued an utterly chilling laugh, but when Glorfindel rode up he fled away into the darkness. When the captain of Gondor returned after regaining control over his horse, Glorfindel warned him not to pursue the Witch-King, saying: "Do not pursue him! He will not return to this land. Far off yet is his doom, and not by the hand of man will he fall."[12] I find it significant that Glorfindel makes this prophesy, the same Glorfindel we met near the Fords of the Bruinen where Frodo was pursued by the nine Black Riders, led by the Witch-King of Angmar.

This prophesy contains such a wonderful twist, as we see in this pivotal scene on the Pelennor Fields. Glorfindel said that the Witch-King would not fall by the hand of man. And throughout the legendarium of Middle-earth, the mortal Children of Ilúvatar are always called Men. Elves and Men. These are the Children of Ilúvatar. The Men of Gondor. The Men of the West. The Men of Rohan. Not only in *The Lord of the Rings*, or only in the English language, but in most languages around the world the masculine term is used to refer to all of humanity, male and female alike. For centuries this masculine usage was unquestioned until only recently, as feminism began to demand a more inclusive term. And it is here, during the Battle of the Pelennor Fields, that this literal emphasis on masculine dominance in both language and culture makes possible the defeat of the Witch-King. For when Dernhelm comes forward as the only Rider still standing to defend the king, the

---

12 Tolkien, *The Return of the King*, "Appendix A," 1027.

Lord of the Nazgûl says: "No living man may hinder me."[13] He too knows the prophesy, and that leads to his undoing: his belief that no mortal can harm him. And then the revelation occurs: Dernhelm is Éowyn, entering battle in *her* despair.

In her felt imprisonment waiting on her uncle, the king, for so many years, her sense of self and autonomy has been shrouded. When she encounters Aragorn for the first time, his charisma and lineage awaken something in her, and she in part projects her own potential upon him in her love and infatuation with him. Yet this is also what leads her on her path to actualize herself, even in her despair as she hopelessly seeks death. But she also seeks honor and renown. And so the prophesy comes true. It is not by the hand of man that the Witch-King meets his downfall. It is, rightfully, at the hands of a woman. So it is that the patriarchal structures, even embedded in language, that for so long confined Éowyn now become her shield, and she is then able to break out of this cage, fulfill her destiny, and come fully into her own.

As is the case with all the great tasks in this tale, this immense feat is not accomplished alone. Merry's courage also awakens, and he stabs the back of the Witch-king's knee with the sword from the Barrow-downs.

---

13 Tolkien, *The Return of the King*, V, vi, 823.

When the four hobbits escaped their imprisonment in the barrow, Merry awakened from a dream or memory possession in which he experienced the death of one of the Men of Westernesse at the hand of one of the Men of Carn Dûm.[14] This memory is from the same wars in the north against Angmar, the Witch-King's realm. The four swords the hobbits receive had been forged for these wars by the Men of Westernesse. Thus, this is the sword Merry carries with him into battle. Both Éowyn's and Merry's swords are destroyed when they touch the undead form of the Witch-king, but they each fulfill their purpose. Here is the passage from that moment:

> So passed the sword of the Barrow-downs, work of Westernesse. But glad would he have been to know its fate who wrought it slowly long ago in the North-kingdom when the Dúnedain were young, and chief among their foes was the dread realm of Angmar and its sorcerer king. No other blade, not though mightier hands had wielded it, would have dealt that foe a wound so bitter, cleaving the undead flesh, breaking the spell that knit his unseen sinews to his will.[15]

---

14 Tolkien, *The Fellowship of the Ring*, I, viii, 140.
15 Tolkien, *The Return of the King*, V, vi, 826.

It seems that Merry has, in this act, fulfilled the unfinished work of the dead—perhaps carrying forward the memory that he experienced in the Barrow-downs, and at last completing the final defeat of Angmar and the terrible Witch-king.

The battle rages on, and the sea breeze carries the next surprise and turn of fate to the Pelennor Fields. When the black sails of the ships, that seem to carry the Corsairs of Umbar, turn to reveal the shining emblem of Elendil on the black background of Aragorn's standard, joy washes over the Rohirrim and the hosts of Gondor. At this point in the story it has been many chapters since we last heard of Aragorn's doings, and his return is unexpected and poignant. How far he has come from being Strider, the shrouded Ranger in the back corner of the inn in Bree. Now his full title is proclaimed as he enters into his homeland at long last, after more than eight decades of preparation.

Despite the deep satisfaction felt when this sixth chapter and the battle come to a close, the seventh chapter, **"The Pyre of Denethor,"** loops back in time once more to pick up Pippin's tale. Here both the extent and the shortcomings of Denethor's knowledge are revealed: what he has seen in the Palantír, and that he believes the war against Sauron will certainly be lost. But he also reveals another reason for his desperate actions:

he has figured out that Aragorn is returning to claim the kingship, and he does not want to surrender his stewardship. If he cannot rule and pass his stewardship on to his son, he would rather take his own life and his son's and have nothing.

At the start of the next chapter, Gandalf acknowledges that Pippin and Merry have each played their vitally important parts during the Battle of the Pelennor: Merry in stabbing the Witch-king and Pippin in saving Faramir's life. His reasons for insisting to Elrond that the two younger hobbits join the Fellowship have been fulfilled.

"The Houses of Healing," the eighth chapter, provides a poignant respite from the intensity of the war and the other conflicts of the story. It takes place at night, in the quiet of the archetypally Lunar realm. This night shows us Aragorn as a healer, while the previous chapter showed him as a warrior. We can see his inner and outer selves, or one might say his archetypal Solar and archetypal Lunar qualities. The healing woman Ioreth says the prophetic words: *"The hands of the king are the hands of a healer. And so the rightful king could ever be known."*[16] We see here themes of the sacral king, the king who is able to bring healing to the land.

---

16 Tolkien, *The Return of the King*, V, viii, 842.

These themes hearken back to the Arthurian legends and beyond even to biblical themes of sacral kingship.[17] The kingship is intimately bound up with healing and wholeness, and with the fruitfulness of the land.

Aragorn's powers of healing come from his lineage as a descendent of Eärendil, one of the half-elven. That is why he says he wishes Elrond was there, as the eldest of all their race. Indeed, as Legolas remarks in the following chapter, Aragorn is one "of the children of Lúthien," the first immortal elf to fall in love with and marry a mortal man.[18] Aragorn's powers for healing are not only his knowledge of herb-lore and the virtues of *athelas*, but also his ability to enter into an altered state of consciousness and, like a shaman, call back the souls of those on the brink of death. When he calls to Faramir, and Éowyn, and Merry, he seems at a remove from those around him, as though he has entered into a different realm as he seeks for them.

I also find it significant that Aragorn comes in his first and most humble form, as Strider, when he comes to the Houses of Healing. As Strider he is most in touch

---

[17] For two essays exploring Aragorn's connection to the Arthurian legends and the themes of sacral kingship, see Verlyn Flieger, "Frodo and Aragorn: The Concept of the Hero" and "Missing Person" in *Green Suns and Faërie: Essays on J. R. R. Tolkien*, 141–158 and 223–231.

[18] Tolkien, *The Return of the King*, V, ix, 858.

with his roots as a Ranger, as a wanderer of the land, intuitively in touch with the natural world. He even jests with Merry about pipeweed when Merry awakens—bridging his noble kingly self with his rogue Ranger identity. Completing the nightly, Lunar themes of this chapter: Aragorn and the sons of Elrond labor through the night healing the sick and wounded. But in the morning, the banner of Dol Amroth flies above the city, and the people wonder if the king's coming was only a dream. Tolkien weaves together all these archetypally Lunar themes of night, healing, and the dream. Aragorn embodies both Lunar and Solar qualities, and shows that a king must not only be a warrior and a leader, but also a healer.

The ninth chapter, **"The Last Debate,"** contains another story within a story. Again, I find it noteworthy whenever Tolkien decides a story should be told in the moment, versus when it should be told again by one of the characters. We hear the tale retold of the Paths of the Dead, and the journey that Gimli and Legolas took with the Grey Company. The Host of the Dead only engage in battle against the Corsairs of Umbar, and their main weapon is fear. As Gimli notes, it is remarkable how the servants of the Dark Lord are overcome by wraiths and fear, which are the Enemy's own weapons. Evil always seems to consume itself in defeat.

Significantly, Aragorn deems the oath of the dead fulfilled after the ships have been conquered and the peoples of the south of Gondor freed to join the battle at Minas Tirith. Thus the Battle of the Pelennor is fought and won entirely by living people rather than by a host of the dead. The land is defended by the people of that land. And the dead are released, finally able to experience the Gift of Ilúvatar and leave the circles of the world at last.

"The Last Debate" concerns what strategic move will defeat Sauron permanently. Gandalf knows this would not rid the world of evil forever, as evil has been woven into the warp and weft of the world from its creation, as told in the *Ainulindalë*. Gandalf says:

> Other evils there are that may come; for Sauron is himself but a servant or emissary. Yet it is not our part to master all the tides of the world, but to do what is in us for the succour of those years wherein we are set, uprooting evil in the fields that we know, so that those who live after may have clean earth to till. What weather they shall have is not ours to rule.[19]

---

19 Tolkien, *The Return of the King*, V, ix, 861.

In some ways Gandalf here echoes his earlier wisdom delivered to Frodo many months earlier back in the Shire: "All we have to decide is what to do with the time that is given us."[20] It also echoes Gandalf's earlier statements to Denethor that he also is a steward: a steward of all of Middle-earth.

"The Last Debate" also concerns the final move to be made in the War of the Ring, one that is simply a distraction—a jest, a feint, a willing bait walking into a trap. This strategy reemphasizes the point Aragorn made in *The Two Towers* when he declared that the true Quest lies with Frodo. Despite risking the annihilation of seven thousand warriors, including, as Gandalf says, the names among them "that are worth more than a thousand mail-clad knights apiece," it is worth the great risk in order to provide Frodo and Sam with the chance to cross Mordor as safely as possible and potentially destroy the Ring.[21] Such a sacrificial move reveals the importance in scale and also the vast collaborative effort that goes into supporting the Quest of the Ring-bearer.

The title of the tenth and final chapter of Book V, **"The Black Gate Opens,"** directly echoes the chapter title from *The Two Towers*, "The Black Gate Is Closed."

---

20 Tolkien, *The Fellowship of the Ring*, I, ii, 50.
21 Tolkien, *The Return of the King*, V, ix, 864.

Tolkien is wonderful at creating these mirrored titles, such as "An Unexpected Party" and "A Long-Expected Party," and "Many Meetings" and, as we will encounter in the final book, "Many Partings."

The journey that the host Aragorn leads to the Black Gate reverses the journey that Frodo, Sam, and Gollum took from the Gate to the Crossroads. We see Ithilien once more but through new eyes. When they arrive at the Gate at last, one can feel the nervousness, fear, and even potential shame of assaulting the Black Land with so small a force. When the Mouth of Sauron comes forth we meet a truly extraordinary figure: "His name is remembered in no tale; for he himself had forgotten it."[22] His identity and sense of self have been completely surrendered to evil and to the will of another. In his encounter with Aragorn they wrestle in the mind. Aragorn strikes a powerful injury, although no physical blows are exchanged. The Mouth of Sauron quails under Aragorn's gaze. Here too we see Aragorn's power extending into the realms of thought.

The tokens that the Mouth of Sauron displays tell us an interesting story, but we do not yet know what has unfolded to bring these items into his hands: Frodo's mithril coat, Sam's sword from the Barrow-downs,

---

22 Tolkien, *The Return of the King*, V, x, 870.

and one of the cloaks of Lothlórien. But in bringing these forward he also reveals more than he perhaps intends. It appears that Sauron knows only of one hobbit, even though the tokens come from both Frodo and Sam. And he refers to him as a spy. And of course he will not produce the prisoner in exchange for the terms he gives, which are worth far more than any prisoner, no matter how mighty or valued. We do not know what has actually happened to Frodo or Sam, but we do know that the whole picture is not being presented, and that Gandalf's shrewd mind is working out all of this.

We see only brief depictions of the battle before the Gate, all portrayed through Pippin's eyes. Miraculously he takes down a troll, before slipping into darkness. We do not know his fate, nor the outcome yet of the battle. Book V ends in as much uncertainty as Book IV. All we know is that the Eagles have come, and yet another echo ricochets between this battle and the Battle of Five Armies at the end of *The Hobbit*.

Tol Erresea

6

The Return of the King – *Book VI*
From Mordor to the Grey Havens

WE HAVE REACHED the final stage of a long, multi-faceted journey. One last time we turn inward, in towards the true Quest of carrying the Ring to Mount Doom. Sam and Frodo's journey into Mordor feels to me like the slowest moving part of the entire narrative, and yet it covers the span of only three chapters. The content is so excruciating, so focused on simply surviving and moving forward through a barren wasteland, that time seems to dilate into a hellish eternity.

When we meet back up with Samwise Gamgee in the opening chapter, **"The Tower of Cirith Ungol,"** we reconnect at exactly the moment we left him at the end of *The Two Towers*. I find it so touching when Sam wonders if the other members of the Fellowship ever think about him and Frodo at all, and we quickly learn where we are in the timeline and that they are not forgotten—even if they are currently beyond help.

The power of the Ring increases immensely right

when Sam crosses the threshold into Mordor and beholds the Mountain of Fire. His visions of what power he might have—as Samwise the Strong, able to transform the realm of Mordor into a vast garden—give us a glimpse of how all who come into possession of the Ring (or are even in proximity to it, as Boromir was) are tempted by it. It makes me wonder what Frodo may have seen in his visions with the Ring—what unfulfilled desires he might have had to tempt him. It is Sam's love for Frodo, and his deep-rooted self-knowledge as a humble hobbit, that saves him from the allure of that vision.

The conflict between the orcs of the Tower of Cirith Ungol and the orcs of Minas Morgul show us once more that evil seems to defeat itself, in a way similar to when the hosts of Sauron were overcome by the fear of the Dead, led by Aragorn. This theme of evil consuming itself symbolically echoes the legends of the First Age about the monstrous spider Ungoliant, who after devouring the light of the Two Trees of Valinor and the numerous gems stolen from the Noldor could no longer sate her insatiable hunger and finally devours herself. In this chapter we see again the theme of evil defeating itself in myriad and subtle ways. The orcs fight each other, destroying the obstacles in Sam's path as he tries to reach Frodo. Even the power granted by the Ring, of cloaking Sam in shadow and an aura of power, protects him from the only orc he directly encounters. The story now reveals how the Mouth of Sauron came to bring the mithril coat, the cloak of Lórien, and the sword of Westernesse to the parley with Gandalf and Aragorn at the Black Gate.

Throughout his climb up the tower, Sam is moved to make decisions by something other than his conscious mind or will. His heart moves him. He intuitively knows he must show the light of the phial of Galadriel to the Watchers at the gate. He knows not to put the Ring back on, even when invisibility might save his life in that moment. He is moved to sing when he cannot find the entrance to the top of the tower. The words "come unbidden."[1] His words of song come from beyond him, a fine example of what Tolkien calls sub-creation. Art comes through the sub-creator from a divine source.

We receive some glimpse of how possessed Frodo is by the Ring when he has the hallucination of Sam as an orc-like creature keeping his treasure from him. Frodo says to Sam: "You can't come between me and this doom."[2] There is a sense in which Frodo is fated to his burden. But if we recall "The Council of Elrond," he takes on the burden freely and willingly.[3] Or so it seems.

---

1 Tolkien, *The Return of the King*, VI, i, 888.
2 Tolkien, *The Return of the King*, VI, i, 891.
3 Tolkien, *The Fellowship of the Ring*, II, ii, 263.

He does have the feeling that some other will is using his voice. So did Frodo choose to be the Ringbearer, or has he stepped into a fate chosen for him long before?

In the crossover between the first and second chapters, Sam and Frodo escape the tower by a hair's breadth. They barely make it. As they leap off the bridge to escape the oncoming orcs coming to the sounding alarm in the tower, the scene echoes one from Dante's *Inferno*. As Dante and Virgil travel through one of the circles of Hell, a host of demons—who speak surprisingly like orcs—come along the road, and Virgil and Dante leap from the road into a hidden ravine—just as Frodo and Sam do.[4] Whether or not this is an intentional echo of Dante on Tolkien's part, I am unsure.

As they continue their journey up the ravine in the chapter **"The Land of Shadow,"** Sam and Frodo witness the changing weather in the clouds far above, and sense that something is shifting in the outer world. They do not know what, although we as the readers know from the earlier accounts of the Battle of the Pelennor Fields.

An exquisite scene, and perhaps one of my personal favorites, takes place when Frodo has gone to sleep and Sam is trying to stay awake. He looks up into the sky

---

4 Dante Alighieri, "Inferno: Canto 23," in *The Divine Comedy*, trans. Robin Kirkpatrick, (London: Penguin, 2012), 101.

and sees beyond the heavy clouds and darkness the piercing beauty of a single star. It is not revealed which star it is, although I like to believe it is Eärendil. The star shines in the west, just as the evening star would. And the hope Sam feels when he sees that celestial orb allows him to surrender to trust and sleep—something he desperately needs for his sanity and survival. The light of Eärendil—the light of the last remaining Silmaril, containing the last remnant of the blended light of the Two Trees of Valinor—aids the Ring Quest in myriad ways: as the light in the star-glass that keeps Shelob at bay, and that also breaks the boundary held by the two Watchers guarding the Tower of Cirith Ungol. And now the light of Eärendil itself gives hope to Sam and affords him some much-needed rest.

As Sam and Frodo take in the sight of the Land of Shadow stretching before them, we learn of how the Dark Power is supported by slavery and tributes from other lands. Sauron's reach extends much more broadly than simply the land of Mordor, and he has enslaved peoples from the south and east. This deepens our understanding of his evil, and how so many of the people in his alleged service are there against their will. This is less a depiction of evil men but rather of men enslaved by a dominating, colonizing power. We also recognize this domination in the conversation between the two orcs who try to track the two hobbits: they hate each other. Each band of orcs is pitted against another, they refer to the Nazgûl as "filthy Shriekers," their talk is considered treasonous, even if it is the truth.[5]

The strange way luck works in Mordor gives the two hobbits at once a blessing and a curse. That they are found by the host of orcs marching north is a curse, but that they are mistaken for orcs themselves is something of a blessing. The gear they have chosen to disguise themselves in tells its own story: those orcs were supposed to be inside Udûn the previous day. If you look at the map, Udûn is the valley in the northwest corner of Mordor where the two mountain ranges meet, where the Black Gate stands. But the name Udûn is far older. Remember when Gandalf calls the Balrog "flame of Udûn"?[6] He does not refer to that northwestern valley in Mordor. He refers to the stronghold of the first Dark Lord, Morgoth, once situated north of Beleriand. This stronghold is more commonly called Utumno, but Udûn is the Sindarin name. This was the origin site of the Balrogs, which is why Gandalf uses the phrase "flame of Udûn." Udûn means "dark pit" or "underworld," and is a synonym for "Hell." The final cursed

---

5 Tolkien, *The Return of the King*, VI, ii, 904.
6 Tolkien, *The Fellowship of the Ring*, II, v, 322.

blessing for the hobbits in this part of the story is that although the march with the orcs is an utterly hellish nightmare, they cover a greater distance across Mordor than if they had struggled along on their own. Their trip is shortened, which is exactly what they needed to preserve their food and reach their destination before the war on the outside took a disastrous turn.

Chapter three, "**Mount Doom**," forms, of course, the culmination, the climax, the fulcrum point of the entire story—yet, the primary center of the narrative action only takes place in the last two or so pages. Most of the chapter details the ongoing struggle to reach the mountain itself, concerned with merely surviving. We have been experiencing the story through Sam's eyes since Frodo was stung by Shelob because Frodo's experience lies beyond anything an ordinary reader could relate to—Sam's perspective is far more relatable. When Sam realizes their food will only take them to their goal, he accepts his own death. This brings a new strength. Giving up hope, he feels his hardened will, determination, and sense of responsibility. He has faced the true prospect of his death and resolves to keep going.

We have some glimpse of how the events of Mount Doom will unfold when Sam offers to carry the Ring for Frodo, and Frodo immediately turns almost violent. He says of the Ring: "I am almost in its power now. I could not give it up, and if you tried to take it I should go mad."[7] How then is he meant to throw it willingly into the fire? Frodo has been robbed of everything, even his memories. There is nothing but the vision of the Ring as a wheel of fire in his waking mind. He can see nothing else. He is in a complete psychological possession state by this object of power, and nothing else exists.

When the hobbits throw away their gear to lighten their load, including Sam's precious cooking gear, I find it interesting that he still keeps the little box given to him by Galadriel. Even though hope has seemingly died in his heart, he keeps this gift and continues to carry it with him into the heart of Mordor.

The affection between the hobbits is so intimate and moving to witness: the way Sam comforts Frodo with his arms and his body. There is such a deep love between them, almost a transcendent love. The scene when Sam carries Frodo always brings me to tears. It is an inversion of the story of Saint Christopher carrying the Christ child across a river. In the Christian legend, the giant Christopher bears travelers through the raging waters of a strong river. One day a little child asks to be borne across the water, and Christopher willingly obliges. Yet as he walks the child becomes heavier and

---

7 Tolkien, *The Return of the King*, VI, iii, 916.

heavier, until he feels he is carrying the weight of the world upon his shoulders. On the river's far bank he sets the child down, and learns that he has borne upon his back no ordinary child but the Christ child. By carrying Christ, Saint Christopher in that moment takes upon himself the heaviness of the world. When Sam carries Frodo though, this scenario reverses. Instead of finding Frodo and the weight of the Ring heavy, Sam finds him surprisingly light. He is able to bear him with little difficulty. We see here how there is no way the Quest of the Ring could have been carried out by an individual alone. Frodo needed Sam every step of the way, and this last, final push more than ever before.

Both Sam and Frodo seem to feel a call, a sense of urgency as they lay panting upon the mountainside, resting their aching bodies for a moment. Their movements appear to be orchestrated in divine timing with the events taking place at the Black Gate. At this final, pivotal moment Gollum returns to the scene. I have always wondered if he too somehow felt that same call that reminded Sam and Frodo of the urgency of their errand. The threads of fate all seem to come together in this moment: the Ring, Frodo, Gollum.

Recall Frodo's prediction in the chapter "The Black Gate Is Closed" in *The Two Towers*, when he foretells the outcome of the Ring's destruction and Sméagol's fate. He warns Sméagol that he is in danger, because he swore his oath on the Ring, and the Ring will twist his oath to his undoing. Frodo declares:

> The desire of it may betray you to a bitter end. You will never get it back. In the last need, Sméagol, I should put on the Precious; and the Precious mastered you long ago. If I, wearing it, were to command you, you would obey, even if it were to leap from a precipice or to cast yourself into the fire. And such would be my command. So have a care, Sméagol![8]

This statement casts a haunting light on what actually unfolds in the heart of Mount Doom. Hints at this abound throughout the tale, as well. Returning all the way to the early chapter "The Shadow of the Past" in *The Fellowship of the Ring*, Gandalf says to Frodo of Gollum: "My heart tells me that he has some part to play yet, for good or ill, before the end; and when that comes, the pity of Bilbo may rule the fate of many—yours not least."[9] Later in *The Return of the King*, Gandalf says to Pippin: "Let us remember that a traitor may betray

---

8 Tolkien, *The Two Towers*, IV, iii, 626.
9 Tolkien, *The Fellowship of the Ring*, I, ii, 58.

himself and do good that he does not intend. It can be so, sometimes."[10]

When Gollum attacks Frodo, and Frodo fights back fiercely, Sam sees the two figures as if in a vision:

> A crouching shape, scarcely more than the shadow of a living thing, a creature now wholly ruined and defeated, yet filled with a hideous lust and rage; and before it stood stern, untouchable now by pity, a figure robed in white, but at its breast it held a wheel of fire. Out of the fire there spoke a commanding voice.
>
> "Begone, and trouble me no more! If you ever touch me again, you shall be cast yourself into the Fire of Doom."[11]

This is no idle threat. As the scene within Sammath Naur unfolds, Frodo's words prove true. Yet what takes place during this encounter between the figure of light and the shape of ruined shadow? The commanding voice comes through the wheel of fire itself. Frodo has grown in stature and in power from resisting his burden, yet he has also gained a certain power from the Ring, as well.

---

10 Tolkien, *The Return of the King*, V, iv, 797.
11 Tolkien, *The Return of the King*, VI, iii, 922.

The will of Frodo, the will of the Ring, and perhaps a will greater than both of them, are all at play during the final dramatic sequence at the Cracks of Doom.

The climactic scene that unfolds between Frodo, Gollum, and the One Ring is an example of what Tolkien calls "eucatastrophe," which he saw as the true "mark of a good fairy-story."[12] Tolkien defines his neologism as the "good catastrophe, the sudden joyous 'turn.'"[13] A eucatastrophe is

> a sudden and miraculous grace: never to be counted on to recur. It does not deny the existence of *dyscatastrophe*, of sorrow and failure: the possibility of these is necessary to the joy of deliverance; it denies (in the face of much evidence, if you will) universal final defeat and in so far is *evangelium*, giving a fleeting glimpse of Joy, Joy beyond the walls of the world, poignant as grief.[14]

The manner in which the scene at the Cracks of Doom unfolds proceeded "simply from the logic of the tale up to that time," as Tolkien remarked in one of his letters.

---

12 Tolkien, *On Fairy-Stories*, 75.

13 Tolkien, *On Fairy-Stories*, 75.

14 Tolkien, *On Fairy-Stories*, 75.

"They were not deliberately worked up to nor foreseen until they occurred."[15] Once again, Tolkien speaks of the progression of the narrative as one who has witnessed it in real time and reported the events, rather than someone simply making up a story plot. He even said he had attempted to sketch out the events in advance, but none of those scenarios "resembled what is actually reported in the finished story."[16] The sudden, joyous turn comes as unexpectedly for the reader, and even the author, as it does for Frodo and Sam.

Despite Frodo's tremendous efforts to the last to resist the temptation of the Ring, once the moment finally comes to cast it into the fire, he has no power left in him to harm the Ring. As he stands with the Ring over the volcanic fires, he has no way forward: he has no will to destroy it, and neither Sam nor anyone else would be able to make him do so. Frodo's only choice is a non-choice; the Ring claims him. "I do not choose now to do what I came to do," Frodo says.[17] "*I do not choose.*" The wording itself is so carefully chosen. His will is overthrown utterly. Frodo is pushed to such an extreme in resisting the Ring that it forces what the

---

15 Tolkien, *Letters*, 325.
16 Tolkien, *Letters*, 325.
17 Tolkien, *The Return of the King*, VI, iii, 924.

depth psychologist C.G. Jung calls an *enantiodromia*: "everything that exists goes over to its opposite."[18] Frodo's goodness has to become evil, and only through that fall into evil can goodness triumph.

Frodo's claiming of the Ring instigates two events: first, Sauron is at last made aware of the designs of his enemies, and he now understands the great danger in which he stands, with the Ring poised on the edge of destruction. In this final moment, Sauron must look inward at himself, at his mistakes and errors, his misjudgments: "the magnitude of his own folly was revealed to him in a blinding flash."[19] Sauron must self-reflect. And in doing so, Sauron's demise and unmaking is already underway. Secondly, Frodo's apparent betrayal creates the conditions for Gollum finally to overpower him. Frodo no longer appears to have the moral superiority, nor the spiritual authority to command Sméagol as he once did. Indeed, only moments prior to Frodo's claiming of the Ring he was able to resist Gollum's latest attack. Yet, by finally wresting the Ring from him, Gollum saves Frodo—his life, and perhaps also his soul,

---

18 C.G. Jung, "Definitions," in *Psychological Types*, vol. 6 of *The Collected Works of C.G. Jung*, trans. R.F.C. Hull, ed. H. Read, M. Fordham, G. Adler, and W. McGuire, Bollingen Series XX, (Princeton, NJ: Princeton UP, 1971), 426, §708.

19 Tolkien, *The Return of the King*, VI, iii, 924.

just as Gandalf predicted in the second chapter of the book. But Gollum's action alone does not complete the Quest. This is the moment chance steps in, making the eucatastrophe complete. The fate of the Ring at the Cracks of Doom seems decided apparently by chance, but it may be that chance indicates a deeper, underlying pattern of meaning.

After Gollum attacks him, Frodo speaks not just a threat, but a prophesy, when he says to Gollum: "If you ever touch me again, you shall be cast yourself into the Fire of Doom."[20] When Gollum bites the Ring from Frodo's hand and holds it up, Sam sees that the Ring "shone now as if verily it was wrought of living fire."[21] The Ring knows it is about to be unmade. It feels the heat of the volcano, before ever touching the magma. The Ring knows its end is near, even before the great chance intervenes. As Gollum gazes upward at the Ring, "he stepped too far, toppled, wavered for a moment on the brink, and then with a shriek he fell. Out of the depths came his last wail *Precious*, and he was gone."[22] This is the final and most utter descent in all of *The Lord of the Rings*: an individual's descent into the fires of Hell, a descent into

---

20 Tolkien, *The Return of the King*, VI, iii, 922.
21 Tolkien, *The Return of the King*, VI, iii, 925.
22 Tolkien, *The Return of the King*, VI, iii, 925.

death—and ensuing rebirth of the whole, a renewal of Middle-earth. Only in the ecstasy of having the Ring in his possession could the wily Gollum have become so unconscious of his surroundings as to fall off the brink, into the magma below. Thus when Gollum and the Ring are reunited, and subsequently when the Ring and the Fire meet, only then can evil be unmade. Good defeats evil not by fighting it outright, but by allowing evil to destroy itself. When evil is brought back to itself, then it is unmade.

But what of Frodo's fate? Some scholars of Tolkien, such as Verlyn Flieger, see Frodo as a failed hero.[23] At one level, the reading of Frodo as a failed hero makes *The Lord of the Rings* an even more poignant, and tragic tale. Yet, as Tolkien himself said, "I do not think that Frodo's was a *moral* failure."[24] Frodo's will has been surrendered to the completion of his task. If the only way to see the Ring destroyed is for Frodo to sacrifice himself—including his own will and goodness—to the task, then that is what he must do. His failure is the only pathway to achievement. Frodo only fails at an individual level; rather his personal will is surrendered to a greater Will. In the terminology of Jungian psychology,

---

23 Flieger, "Missing Person," 229.
24 Tolkien, *Letters*, 326.

he has surrendered his ego and given himself up to the Self. Frodo becomes an instrument of a higher power, by giving up everything that remains of his individual self—which was his capacity to resist the Ring. Frodo's surrender creates the conditions for the Quest to be fulfilled in the only way that it could.

So, is Frodo a failed hero? Or might I suggest, that when Frodo finally gives himself to the Ring, does he not become as Christ on the cross, surrendering at last to his doubt and the bitterness of the full human condition, believing God has in the end abandoned him? Is Frodo any more of a failed hero than Christ? And is it not through that failure, that Christ redeems all sins, and Frodo's Quest is achieved? This may be the true meaning of "eucatastrophe." As Tolkien writes in "On Fairy-Stories":

> The peculiar quality of the "joy" of successful Fantasy can thus be explained as a sudden glimpse of the underlying reality or truth.... But in the "eucatastrophe" we see in brief vision that the answer may be greater—it may be a far-off gleam or echo of *evangelium* in the real world.[25]

---

25 Tolkien, *On Fairy-Stories*, 77.

The eucatastrophe of every fantasy, of every fairy-story, recalls the eucatastrophe of the Gospels: "The Birth of Christ is the eucatastrophe of Man's history. The Resurrection is the eucatastrophe of the story of the Incarnation."[26] The eucatastrophe is composed not only of the turn towards joy, the miraculous grace, but out of that which it turns from: the failure. The failure is necessary for the eucatastrophe to be complete. The eucatastrophe of *The Lord of the Rings* is an enantiodromia, a great reversal of one extreme into its opposite: evil is turned to good, and failure is turned to sudden deliverance.

From the end of this moment onward, the remaining chapters serve primarily to close the loose ends of the story. The many narrative threads reunite slowly. Chapter four, **"The Field of Cormallen"** reconnects with the battle at the Black Gate, and then the Eagles rescue Frodo and Sam from the collapsing mountainside. Tolkien tried to deploy the Eagles as a device as sparingly as possible: for rescue when no other hope exists, but never to intervene overmuch.

When the hobbits awaken in the field of Cormallen, they find themselves in unexpected positions of honor. Even their ragged clothes are hallowed, now revered. Their task has sanctified everything they carried into

---

[26] Tolkien, *On Fairy-Stories*, 78.

the heart of Mordor. As Sam awakens and is greeted by Gandalf, this scene echoes the moment in Rivendell when Frodo awakens after crossing the Fords. In both scenes Gandalf reorients the hobbits to the day and time—contextualizing the extremity and timelessness of their adventure back into the timely rhythms of the mundane world.

Frodo's resistance to wearing a sword at the feast is a symbol of the pacifism that has been instilled in him. Even before the events at Mount Doom he said he did not believe it would be his part to strike a blow again. This attitude carries forward to the events that unfold in the penultimate chapter, "The Scouring of the Shire," and Frodo's desire to keep the hobbits from fighting at all costs.

The Ring was destroyed on March 25, a significant date in the Christian calendar: the celebration of the Annunciation, when the angel Gabriel tells the Virgin Mary she will be the mother of God. Tolkien writes that the hobbits and the Men of Gondor stay in Ithilien until it is almost May—over a month passes before they return to Minas Tirith. Time in the story dilates again.

In the fifth chapter, **"The Steward and the King,"** the story turns back to pick up the tales of Faramir and Éowyn. Earlier, in the chapter "The Houses of Healing," we came to a deeper understanding of Éowyn, recognizing her pain and despair. Aragorn, Éomer, and Gandalf each have distinct perspectives on what ails her, but Gandalf perhaps sees her more clearly than any other. Gandalf speaks of how being born as a woman has confined her to duties that did not match her spirit and courage. Furthermore, the poisonous words spoken by Wormtongue would have affected her deeply. Such extraordinary lines, when Gandalf says: "But who knows what she spoke to the darkness, alone, in the bitter watches of the night, when all her life seemed shrinking, and the walls of her bower closing in about her, a hutch to trammel some wild thing in?"[27] No wonder she wanted to break free, even shirking her duty to lead her people. When one spends her whole life captive to duty, rebellion is all the more likely.

The softly budding romance between Faramir and Éowyn brings some healing to her wounds. She has already achieved something beyond glorious, defeating the Witch-king. But it has not brought the wholeness she was seeking. She still longs for Aragorn, for what she has projected of herself upon the image of him.

As Faramir and Éowyn stand upon the walls of the city looking East at the moment of the great eucatastrophe—when the Ring is destroyed and Sauron

---

27 Tolkien, *The Return of the King*, V, viii, 849.

falls—Faramir says it reminds him of Númenor. He says he often dreams of the Great Wave and the foundering of Númenor. I have mentioned the tale of the drowning of Númenor a number of times, but the original source of this tale stems from a recurring dream Tolkien had, beginning in childhood and continuing throughout much of his adult life. He called this powerful, recurring dream his "Atlantis-haunting." Here is how Tolkien described it in one of his letters:

> This legend or myth or dim memory of some ancient history has always troubled me. In sleep I had the dreadful dream of the ineluctable Wave, either coming out of the quiet sea, or coming in towering over the green inlands. It still occurs occasionally, though now exorcized by writing about it. It always ends by surrender, and I wake gasping out of deep water.[28]

Tolkien wrote of the Great Wave again and again throughout his life. In each telling, the inescapable wave destroys a great civilization, a vast abyss opening in the sea and swallowing an inhabited island in all its glory. Although the dream had haunted him since

---

28 Tolkien, *Letters*, 347.

childhood, Tolkien did not compose his first written telling of the Great Wave, originally titled *The Fall of Númenor*, until 1936. This narrative was penned in conjunction with, and initially intended to be the ending of, Tolkien's unfinished time-travel narrative, *The Lost Road*. That story begins in contemporary England and moves backward through history by means of dream and familially-inherited memory. Tolkien left *The Lost Road* unfinished, moving on instead to write *The Lord of the Rings* as a sequel to *The Hobbit*. Yet in the mid-1940s Tolkien picked up the narrative of the Great Wave and Númenor again in a different frame: *The Notion Club Papers*, the multi-layered story of an Oxford literary group, modeled upon the Inklings.

Tolkien speculated that what he called his "Atlantis complex," his recurring dream of the Great Wave, might possibly have been inherited from his parents.[29] In a letter from the 1950s he writes: "Possibly inherited, though my parents died too young for me to know such things about them, and too young to transfer such things by words. Inherited from me (I suppose) by one only of my children, though I did not know that about my son until recently, and he did not know it about

---

29 Tolkien, *Letters*, 213.

me."[30] In another letter from the same period Tolkien remarks: "That vision and dream has been ever with me—and has been inherited (as I only discovered recently) by one of my children."[31] That child was his second son, Michael.

First in *The Lost Road* and then in *The Notion Club Papers*, Tolkien was attempting to find a literary home for his inundating dream experience of the Great Wave. The fall of Númenor was Tolkien's "personal alteration of the Atlantis myth," the story of the drowning of an advanced island civilization that entered the Western written tradition through Plato's *Timaeus*.[32] The vision had an ongoing and powerful grip upon Tolkien throughout the entirety of his life. He wrote:

> Of all the mythical or "archetypal" images this is the one most deeply seated in my imagination, and for many years I had a recurrent Atlantis dream: the stupendous and ineluctable wave advancing from the Sea or over the land, sometimes dark, sometimes green and sunlit.[33]

---

[30] The son who inherited the dream of the Great Wave is Tolkien's second eldest child, Michael (Tolkien, *Letters*, 213).

[31] Tolkien, *Letters*, 232.

[32] Tolkien, *Letters*, 361.

[33] Tolkien, *Letters*, 361.

In the climax of *The Notion Club Papers*, several members of the group experience themselves simultaneously in Oxford and at the drowning of Númenor. Not only are these individuals vividly present in the distant and seemingly mythic past, but the events of the cataclysm burst through into their current moment, bringing the Great Storm of 1987 crashing onto England's shores. The fictional 2012 editor of the Notion Club Papers comments how remarkable it is that although seemingly written in the 1940s the papers accurately predict the Great Storm of Thursday, June 12, 1987. The editor comments:

> I am now convinced that the papers are a work of fiction; and it may well be that the predictions (notably of the Storm), though genuine and not coincidences, were unconscious: giving one more glimpse of the strange processes of so-called literary "invention," with which the Papers are largely concerned.[34]

Now, a remarkable synchronicity exists here: within the fictional story of *The Notion Club Papers*, the Great Storm of 1987 is predicted, and it is stated to be precognitive. What is amazing, is that a great storm actually

---

34 Tolkien, "The Notion Club Papers," 158.

took place in England in 1987. Christopher Tolkien has noted that "my father's 'prevision' was only out by four months. The greatest storm in living memory struck southern England, causing vast damage, on October 16th, 1987."[35] So not only within the story is the vision of the Great Wave precognitive, but in actual fact Tolkien seems to have predicted the storm that wreaked havoc on England's shores in 1987, an event that occurred well after he had passed away. So many mysterious layers to this precognitive vision persist.

Tolkien had been haunted by this dream for many years, and had written about it in myriad forms. Yet when he bestowed the dream upon Faramir—or perhaps recognized Faramir to be the true dreamer of this vision—the Great Wave at last ceased to return to Tolkien. He even felt that doing so had released a "hidden 'complex.'" Tolkien went on to say: "when Faramir speaks of his private vision of the Great Wave, he speaks for me."[36] Which is what we see here in this scene between Faramir and Éowyn, as they watch the great shadow rise and disperse in the moment of Sauron's defeat.

Faramir's approach to falling in love with Éowyn is so beautiful and moving because he does not require

---

35 Christopher Tolkien, ed., "The Notion Club Papers," 211, n. 1.
36 Tolkien, *Letters*, 232.

her to be anything other than who she is. He sees her deeds and recognizes her beauty. He says he would even love her if she were the blissful Queen of Gondor, married to Lord Aragorn. Faramir's true confession of his love for Éowyn lets her understand her own heart. I find it significant that the first thing she says is "I stand in Minas Anor, the Tower of the Sun."[37] The Sun is an archetypal symbol of one's identity and sense of self. She had been projecting her Solar identity onto Aragorn, and she also sought it in death on the battlefield, since she could not find it within herself. But to have who she truly is reflected back to her by Faramir—who has a more Lunar, empathic, intuitive, healing nature—she can at last own her Solar self. The pair of them form a syzygy, a union of Solar and Lunar, in which she embodies the Solar and he the Lunar—as is fitting for a tale in which the Sun is feminine and the Moon masculine.

The ceremony of Aragorn's crowning brings together the high and low, elevating to a regal level what in the earlier parts of the story were familiar and earthy: his role as Strider alchemically transformed into King Elessar, and mentions of such memories of him rising out of the grass in the plains of Rohan when Éomer first saw him. Also it is fitting that that of all

---

37 Tolkien, *The Return of the King*, VI, v, 943.

characters it should be Gandalf who crowns him: funny old Gandalf the Grey who smokes pipeweed in the Shire, now transformed into the highest power in the land, able to bestow the crown on the rightful king. We see how legends are made, as the old woman Ioreth tells of Frodo's deed—not as crawling, almost helpless through the dust of Mordor, but rather of doing battle with Sauron himself.

Aragorn brings peace and healing to the land, reminiscent of the symbol of the sacral king. Rather than defeating the people of other countries, even those in league with Sauron, he pardons them and makes peace. The lands are restored to freedom and fertility. But something more is needed to complete his kingship. He is waiting for a sign. I so appreciate Gandalf's statement: "Many folk like to know beforehand what is to be set on the table; but those who have laboured to prepare the feast like to keep their secret; for wonder makes the words of praise louder."[38] Now we can have some understanding of why Gandalf kept so much secret or hidden—not only for safety of information, but also for the delight in wonder: such as when he refrains from revealing the defeat of Saruman, instead leading Théoden and the others to witness it themselves.

---

38 Tolkien, *The Return of the King*, VI, v, 949.

The scene when Gandalf and Aragorn climb above Minas Tirith on the slopes of Mount Mindolluin is both poignant and richly symbolic. Aragorn worries that his line will end with him, if his wish is not granted: that Arwen might be his wife and queen. Many years before, Elrond denied him this wish. Unless Aragorn were to come into the inheritance of his kingdom, Elrond would not give up his daughter—who would be relinquishing her own immortality and staying in Middle-earth instead of departing for Eldamar in the West. Only if Arwen would be queen of the North and South kingdoms and could restore the line of Númenor and the children of Lúthien would Elrond consent; he would not want her to marry anyone less than the king of the reunited realm.

The story of Aragorn and Arwen is told in Appendix A, and of all the material in the appendices, this is the one most worth reading. It tells of how Aragorn first saw Arwen when he was only twenty years old, and believed her to be Lúthien Tinúviel, of whom he had been singing as he wandered in the woods. Seeing her, he thought he was seeing a vision of the song he was singing, for their encounter echoes that of Beren seeing Lúthien dancing in the forest of Doriath—which echoes Tolkien watching his wife Edith dance in the woods of Yorkshire. Many years later Arwen and

Aragorn meet in Lothlórien, and they betroth themselves to each other—renouncing the Shadow and the Twilight—renouncing both Sauron and the Undying West. But it is almost another forty years before their marriage is able to come to fruition.

The sapling Aragorn finds on the slopes of Mount Mindolluin is a descendent of the tree Galathilion, a tree in the Blessed Realm made in the image of the silver tree of Valinor, the tree whose final flower became the Moon. The sapling is only seven years old, even though it was likely planted centuries before. This is the sign he has been looking for, the sign that bestows the blessing of the land itself on his reign. Thus the full significance of Aragorn's name—which means Lord of the Tree—is revealed. When Arwen, the Evenstar of her people, comes to Minas Tirith to wed Aragorn, Frodo makes a significant statement: "Now not day only shall be beloved, but night too shall be beautiful and blessed and all its fear pass away."[39] The Evenstar hallows the night, and returns it to the state that Tom Bombadil mentioned near the beginning of the story: "He knew the dark under the stars when it was fearless—before the Dark Lord came from Outside."[40]

---

39 Tolkien, *The Return of the King*, VI, v, 951.
40 Tolkien, *The Fellowship of the Ring*, I, vii, 129.

Chapters six and seven, **"Many Partings"** and "Homeward Bound," carry the four hobbits from Gondor all the way back to the edge of the Shire. Just as the members of the Fellowship came together one by one in the opening of the story, now they go their separate ways and are left behind. The most tragic parting is between Arwen and her father Elrond: "bitter was their parting that should endure beyond the ends of the world."[41]

When the group of travelers comes to the Treegarth of Isengard and encounter Treebeard, he says at the parting from Galadriel and Celeborn that he does not think they will meet again. While Celeborn says he does not know, Galadriel gives a curious response: "Not in Middle-earth, nor until the lands that lie under the wave are lifted up again. Then in the willow-meads of Tasarinan we may meet in the Spring."[42] Tasarinan was a region of Beleriand that does indeed lie beneath the waves. But what does Galadriel mean? She seems almost to be saying they will meet again when the cycle of the world is renewed, after the great end and a new beginning. She speaks of a cyclical, mythical view of history.

---

41 Tolkien, *The Return of the King*, VI, vi, 956.
42 Tolkien, *The Return of the King*, VI, vi, 959.

When they encounter the ruined Saruman on the road, he says: "You have doomed yourselves and you know it. And it will afford me some comfort as I wander to think that you pulled down your own house when you destroyed mine."[43] What does he mean? He is speaking to Elrond and Galadriel, as two of the bearers of the Elven Rings of Power. By destroying the One Ring, the power of the Three Rings has also ended. Everything they made through those Rings—the timelessness of Lothlórien, the deep memory of Rivendell—will now fade with the passage of time. The time of the Elves is indeed now over. In the final days that Galadriel, Celeborn, Elrond, and Gandalf all have together, they speak of many things. But Tolkien's description indicates that they do not speak with words, but rather directly from mind to mind—yet another example of the subtle magic of this world.

When they come at last back to Rivendell, Bilbo gives Frodo something quite important: three books of lore that he had made, "labelled on their red backs: *Translations from the Elvish, by B.B.*"[44] Why is this so important? These three red volumes are to be included with the book that started as Bilbo's diary, and will

---

43 Tolkien, *The Return of the King*, VI, vi, 961.
44 Tolkien, *The Return of the King*, VI, vi, 964.

soon come to contain Frodo's narrative telling of his journey and the War of the Ring. These volumes all together form *The Red Book of Westmarch*. Those three books of lore tell the stories we would find in *The Silmarillion*. This is significant because this is the pretense of how we as readers come to have these books in our hands. The transcribers and redactors of the stories are part of the stories themselves.

At the end of the chapter "Many Partings," Bilbo sings the familiar song which begins with the lines "The Road goes ever on and on."[45] Each time this song is sung, whether by Bilbo or Frodo, it has slightly different words, which indicate how they are each faring in their lives.

The first time this poem is recited is actually in the final chapter of *The Hobbit*, when Bilbo is returning from his adventures to the Shire. In this version the opening line of each verse is "Roads go ever on and on."[46] He is summarizing his adventures in these verses, and speaking to the many roads he has traveled.

This verse appears for the first time in *The Lord of the Rings* at the end of the very first chapter, as Bilbo is leaving Bag End. He says the lines:

---

45 Tolkien, *The Return of the King*, VI, vi, 965.
46 Tolkien, *The Hobbit*, 313.

Now far ahead the Road has gone,
And I must follow, if I can,
Pursuing it with eager feet,
Until it joins some larger way.[47]

This verse appears a second time in the third chapter of *The Fellowship of the Ring*, and it is now Frodo singing the words as he departs on his own journey. The lines are almost identical to Bilbo's, but instead of saying "Pursuing it with eager feet," Frodo says "Pursuing it with weary feet."[48] We see the different nature of their adventures just in the exchange of the word "eager" for "weary."

The verse appears for a third time at the end of this chapter "Many Partings" in *The Return of the King*, and again it is Bilbo singing the song. But now the words have been changed even more. Bilbo sings:

Now far ahead the Road has gone,
Let others follow it who can!
Let them a journey new begin,
But I at last with weary feet
Will turn towards the lighted inn,
My evening-rest and sleep to meet.[49]

---

47 Tolkien, *The Fellowship of the Ring*, I, i, 35.
48 Tolkien, *The Fellowship of the Ring*, I, iii, 72.
49 Tolkien, *The Return of the King*, VI, vi, 965.

In these differing lines we can perceive how Bilbo's journey is coming to a true close, and that he will soon depart Middle-earth forever. His life is nearing its end.

The last three chapters of the book in themselves comprise their own narrative arc. Just as we feel the whole story coming to a close and everything settling back in to how it was before—or as Frodo says, that it "feels more like falling asleep again"—we realize it is not quite finished.[50] The chapter **"Homeward Bound"** intimates that not all has been well in Bree and in the Shire. But the penultimate chapter, **"Scouring of the Shire"** carries a pivotal twist that is essential to the full unfolding of the story. When the hobbits come home to find the Shire destroyed by industrialization, it undermines the usual hero arc of the journey and the return. Instead of returning to a peaceful homeland, the fields have been laid waste, the beautiful hobbit-holes destroyed and replaced with hideously efficient brick buildings, large mills have been erected and pour black smoke in the air and foul sewage in the rivers, and beloved trees have been cut for firewood or left to rot. Tolkien is clearly making a commentary on industrial capitalism in this chapter. The feeling when the hobbits return to the Shire is that of veterans who have fought

---

50 Tolkien, *The Return of the King*, VI, vii, 974.

abroad returning to a homeland ravaged by war. The hobbits—particularly Merry, Pippin, and Sam—have learned all that they need in their journeys to have the authority and power to contend with the discord they find at home. And Frodo has his own important role to play, as a peacekeeper: he has seen enough of evil, and reminds the others that no hobbit has ever killed another intentionally in the Shire, and it will not begin then.

We see here the final end of Saruman, who certainly seems to deserve the fate that comes to him. It is shocking to see how low he has fallen, intentionally destroying the Shire purely out of spite for the hobbits and Gandalf. He even attempts to murder Frodo, despite that it would serve no purpose for himself or any greater cause. That Saruman falls at Wormtongue's hand is the final example of evil destroying itself.

To heal the hurts of this techno-industrial ravaging, the community of the Shire draws on their hidden strength and courage that is awakened only by dire need. They undertake the task of healing the land, re-sowing the fields and nourishing the soils, replanting trees and tending them with loving care. The work of restoring and healing the Shire is not done by a solo hero acting alone, it is accomplished by a community working together. Sam's gift from Galadriel, of the soil from her garden and the *mallorn* seed, which he carried with him into the core of Mordor, are a symbol of the hope that never really died in his heart. She knew he would need this gift to regenerate the Shire.

The final chapter, "**The Grey Havens,**" is exquisitely bittersweet. The emotional tone of this chapter perfectly captures the Elvish sorrow and longing to which Tolkien was privy and able to articulate in language. Even as all the threads of the story are coming together, and Sam's life is coming into fruition—all his wishes coming true as he says—there is still the sacrifice and tragedy of Frodo. He is still wounded, and cannot find peace in the Shire.

Before Frodo departs, he gives *The Red Book* to Sam, an important transition—the means by which the story will eventually come to us.

When Frodo and Sam set out on their last journey together, Frodo sings a familiar walking song—one that he, Sam, and Pippin sang together in the chapter "Three Is Company" near the beginning of *The Fellowship of the Ring*. That earlier song was much longer, with several verses. The most important lines from that first song are these:

> *Still round the corner there may wait*
> *A new road or a secret gate,*
> *And though we pass them by today,*

> *Tomorrow we may come this way*
> *And take the hidden paths that run*
> *Towards the Moon or to the Sun.*[51]

Frodo repeats a slight variation of these lines when he and Sam pass through the autumn woods, right before they encounter the Elves traveling towards the Grey Havens. Frodo sings:

> *Still round the corner there may wait*
> *A new road or a secret gate;*
> *And though I oft have passed them by,*
> *A day will come at last when I*
> *Shall take the hidden paths that run*
> *West of the Moon, East of the Sun.*[52]

Those last lines about the hidden paths that run West of the Moon, East of the Sun, echo a trope in many fairy-stories. Indeed, the realm of Faërie is said to be West of the Moon, East of the Sun. And Tolkien even used these lines in one of his earliest poems of Middle-earth, titled "The Shores of Faery," written in 1915. The opening lines of that poem are:

---

51 Tolkien, *The Fellowship of the Ring*, I, iii, 76.
52 Tolkien, *The Return of the King*, VI, ix, 1005.

> *East of the Moon*
> *West of the Sun*
> *There stands a lonely hill*
> *Its feet are in the pale green Sea*
> *Its towers are white & still.*[53]

Here the directions are reversed, "East of the Moon, West of the Sun," instead of "West of the Moon, East of the Sun." But they carry the same meaning. This is a place beyond the confines of this mundane world. The final verse of "The Shores of Faery" repeats these lines again:

> *O West of the Sun, East of the Moon*
> *Lies the Haven of the Star*
> *The white tower of the Wanderer,*
> *And the rocks of Eglamar,*
> *There Vingelot is harboured*
> *While Earéndel looks afar*
> *On the magic and the wonder*
> *'Tween here and Eglamar*
> *Out, out, beyond Taniquetil*
> *In Valinor – afar.*[54]

---

53 Tolkien, as quoted in Hammond and Scull, *Artist & Illustrator*, 47.
54 Tolkien, as quoted in Hammond and Scull, *Artist & Illustrator*, 48.

The whole mythology of Middle-earth is incapsulated in this early 1915 poem in some ways. Thus is it fitting that Tolkien's great work, his magnum opus, his masterwork, *The Lord of the Rings*, should end where it all began. With a mariner sailing west, just as Eärendil did in the first verse Tolkien ever wrote of Middle-earth, and now as the Ringbearers do in the last story of Middle-earth. The mythology is book-ended by this voyage west, this voyage to the Undying Realm—to Faërie.

Now we can recognize the full meaning of the name Elf-friend, as bestowed upon Frodo by Gildor when he first set out on his journey. Both Frodo and Bilbo are Elf-friends, not only because of their close relationships with the Elves, but also because they too cross out of this mortal world and pass into the Undying Lands. Tolkien first began to write of Middle-earth with the story of a mariner named Ælfwine who sailed into the West and heard the stories of the Elves, recording them in *The Golden Book of Tavrobel*. Ælfwine is a witness and traveler between realms. And now Tolkien's legendarium comes to a close with Frodo and Bilbo sailing West, and leaving behind them their stories as recorded in *The Red Book of Westmarch*. The tale comes full circle at last, and is complete.

We learn now that Gandalf was the bearer of the third of the Elven Rings, and he departs over the Sea with the other two Elven Ringbearers. The Rings of Power defined the Third Age, and now with the passing of that age, their time and power has ended as well.

The parting between Frodo and the other three hobbits, particularly between Frodo and Sam, is perhaps the most heartbreaking moment of this story. I will never forget, at thirteen years old, how hard I cried reading the end of this book. I knew then that this was what great stories were made of: not only the triumph of the eucatastrophe, but the inevitable bittersweet loss at the end. It still moves me to tears, every time I read this ending. There is perhaps some vindication to know—which we can learn from the Tale of Years in Appendix B—that at the end of his long life, and after his wife Rosie passes away, Samwise Gamgee does take a ship and sails the Straight Road west—for he too was a Ringbearer. And indeed, Legolas and Gimli are also afforded that honor—Legolas because he is an Elf, and Gimli as a favor from Galadriel. But these are pieces of an after story and a history, not the conclusion to this particular tale. Frodo sails over the Sea to find healing—not immortality, as some have interpreted, but simply to find rest from his labors and healing for his deep wounds.[55] And that

---

55 Tolkien, *Letters*, 328.

is where the sweetness dwells in this bitter parting. Frodo at last can come to the peace he has earned. He has sacrificed himself for Middle-earth, and though he must depart it so that he can return to wholeness, he leaves behind the healing and wholeness that his great labor has afforded. As was foreseen in his dream of the Sea in Crickhollow, and his dream in the house of Tom Bombadil and Goldberry, Frodo crosses the threshold of this world and arrives at the white shores of Elvenhome.

When Sam returns home, he says the immortal lines: "Well, I'm back."[56] Some say these are some of the most tragic lines uttered in literature. For one can read them in several ways. He says: "Well, I'm back," indicating he has returned. But they could also be read "Well, *I'm* back," with the emphasis that he has returned even though others have not.[57] It is a line acknowledging those who have died in the great battles of the War of the Ring, and also acknowledging the departure of the Ringbearers, and most importantly Frodo. "'Well, I'm back,' he said."

---

56 Tolkien, *The Return of the King*, VI, ix, 1008.

57 I credit Verlyn Flieger for this especially poignant reading of Sam's final lines. Verlyn Flieger, "Gilson, Smith, and Baggins," in *Green Suns and Faërie: Essays on J. R. R. Tolkien*, 282.

Thus, at last, Book VI of *The Return of the King* comes to a close. Our journey together into the imaginal realm comes to an end. And yet, just like Frodo departing over the Sea, it is also a new beginning. For the path to Faërie is always open to those who know how to find the entrance, and J.R.R. Tolkien has left us an extraordinary map to follow.

Epilogue

I CAN RECALL AS CLEARLY as if it were yesterday what it was like to finish reading *The Lord of the Rings* for the first time. I was sitting at my desk, holding the pages open with both hands. I remember how the light fell across the pages of the book. I could barely see the words, because tears were falling in heavy droplets from my eyes. I made sure to lean back, so the splashing teardrops would not stain the pages of this precious book. I had never been so touched by a story before, and I honestly have not been to the same degree since. From that moment, I have been trying to understand why I was so deeply affected by these words penned by J. R. R. Tolkien.

Not everyone has such a profound experience of this book, although I have now had the joy of meeting many who have. One has a feeling of recognition when encountering such an individual. There is a mutual feeling, a sense that we both have "been there" before. Perhaps such a feeling is not dissimilar from meeting someone who has traveled to the same unique part of the world as you, or been at the same meaningful event, but you only happen to meet years later. The feeling is: "Oh—you know, too, don't you?"

I had that first experience of reading *The Lord of the Rings* at age thirteen, and I continued to reread it each year until the beginning of my twenties. I have since learned many individuals do this, almost like a ritual, returning to a sacred text again and again. I have also met numerous people who first heard this tale spoken aloud, read to them by a parent, a friend, or a lover. The text comes alive when spoken, and it continues an oral tradition of story-telling within which I believe Tolkien would have wanted to situate his story. After all, *The Lord of the Rings* was read aloud in draft to the Inklings, and commented upon by Tolkien's close friends and children as it was being composed. It is only fitting that the story should continue to be shared through spoken voice, giving lilt and song to the dialogue and the breath of life to the exquisite narrative descriptions.

I did reach an age when I thought I had to set *The Lord of the Rings* and other such fairy-stories aside. I figured I had to grow out of such childish things eventually. But even when I tried, Middle-earth stayed with me. I found I could not leave this land that I could access through my imagination. Thus, I was given a tremendous gift when a professor of mine in graduate school assigned Tolkien's essay "On Fairy-Stories," and I realized I could study this material as an adult. Suddenly a vast world opened up before me, and I was driven by an intense curiosity to understand what the imagination is and how it is possible to have such immersive internal experiences. The more I have delved into this material the more I have come to see the imagination as a source of knowledge, wisdom, and even truth, and the imaginal realm as a real place. Affirming the imaginal experiences of others, experiences that often mirrored those I had when reading *The Lord of the Rings*, has been one of my greatest joys since engaging with this work. I have learned that the imagination, far from being something unreal or simply made up, is a powerful, animating source, permeating the physical world and connecting it to the spiritual world. Gaston Bachelard writes:

> The imagination is a tree. It has the integrative virtues of a tree. It is root and boughs. It lives between earth and sky. It lives in the earth and in the wind. The imagined tree becomes imperceptibly the cosmological tree, the tree which epitomizes the universe, which makes a universe....[1]

1 Gaston Bachelard, *On Poetic Imagination and Reverie* (Putnam, CT: Spring, 2005), 85.

The imagination connects us to the whole cosmos, linking matter, psyche, and spirit. There is no age at which we are meant to set this aside. Imagination comes innately to children, but that does not mean it is only for children. The time has come for us to trust the imaginal once more, to reclaim that child-like wonder as mature adults. Such experiences are our birthright as human beings, as denizens of this living cosmos. The path is always there for us, if we choose to seek it. As Bilbo says, there is only one Road, but every path is its tributary.[2] All we need to do is step out our front doorway and cross that threshold, and there is no knowing where it may take us.

---

[2] Tolkien, *The Fellowship of the Ring*, I, iii, 72.

Bibliography

Alighieri, Dante. *The Divine Comedy*, translated by Robin Kirkpatrick. London: Penguin, 2012.

Bachelard, Gaston. *On Poetic Imagination and Reverie*. Putnam, CT: Spring, 2005.

Carpenter, Humphrey. *J.R.R. Tolkien: A Biography*. New York: Houghton Mifflin, 2000.

Coleridge, Samuel Taylor. *Biographia Literaria*. London: J.M. Dent, 1906.

Corbin, Henry. "*Mundus Imaginalis*, or The Imaginary and the Imaginal." Translated by Ruth Horine. *Spring: An Annual of Archetypal Psychology and Jungian Thought* (1972). https://pdfs.semanticscholar.org/ob1c/ecef17498852e164b3ef36dcd071fccf1cf7.pdf.

D'Ardenne, Simone. "The Man and Scholar." In *J.R.R. Tolkien, Scholar and Storyteller: Essays in Memoriam*, edited by Mary Salu and Robert T. Farrell. Ithaca, NY: Cornell UP, 1979.

Edwards, Raymond. *Tolkien*. London: Robert Hale, 2014.

Flieger, Verlyn. *A Question of Time: J.R.R. Tolkien's Road to Faërie*. Kent, OH: The Kent State UP, 1997.

———. "But What Did He Really Mean?" *Tolkien Studies* 11 (2014): 149-66.

———. *Green Suns and Faërie: Essays on J.R.R. Tolkien*. Kent, OH: The Kent State UP, 2012.

———. *Splintered Light: Logos and Language in Tolkien's World*. Kent, OH: The Kent State UP, 2002.

Fry, Carrol. "'Two Musics about the Throne of Ilúvatar': Gnostic and Manichaean Dualism in *The Silmarillion*." *Tolkien Studies* 12 (2015): 77-93.

Fussell, Paul. *The Great War and Modern Memory*. New York: Oxford UP, 2013.

Garth, John. *Tolkien and the Great War: The Threshold of Middle-Earth*. New York: Houghton Mifflin, 2003.

Godwin, Joscelyn. "Tolkien and the Primordial Tradition." Paper given at the Second International Conference on the Fantastic in the Arts, at Florida Atlantic University, March 18-21, 1981. https://hermetic.com/godwin/tolkien-and-the-primordial-tradition.

Hammond, Wayne G. and Christina Scull. *J.R.R. Tolkien: Artist & Illustrator*. New York: Houghton Mifflin, 2000.

Jeffrey, David Lyle. "Tolkien as Philologist." In *Tolkien and the Invention of Myth*, edited by Jane Chance, 61-78. Lexington: The University Press of Kentucky, 2004.

Jung, C.G. 1976. "The Concept of the Collective Unconscious." In *The Portable Jung*, edited by Joseph Campbell, translated by R.F.C. Hull, 59-69. New York: Penguin.

———. "Definitions." In *Psychological Types*. Vol. 6 of *The Collected Works of C.G. Jung*, translated by R.F.C. Hull, edited by H. Read, M. Fordham, G. Adler, and W. McGuire, 408-86. Bollingen Series XX. Princeton, NJ: Princeton UP, 1971.

Lewis, C.S. "Professor J.R.R. Tolkien: Creator of Hobbits and Inventor of a New Mythology." In *J.R.R. Tolkien, Scholar and Storyteller: Essays in Memoriam*, edited by Mary Salu and Robert T. Farrell. Ithaca, NY: Cornell University, 1979.

McIlwaine, Catherine. *Tolkien: Maker of Middle-earth*. Oxford: Bodleian Library, 2018.

Noel, Ruth S. *The Languages of Tolkien's Middle-Earth*. Boston: Houghton Mifflin, 1974.

Owens, Lance. S. "Jung and Tolkien: The Hermeneutics of Vision." Lecture hosted by the Philosophy, Cosmology, and Consciousness Forum, presented at the California Institute of Integral Studies, San Francisco, CA, October 23, 2015. https://pccforum.wordpress.com/2015/10/13/lance-owens-md-jung-tolkien-and-the-hermeneutics-of-vision/.

———. "Lecture I: The Discovery of Faërie." In "J.R.R. Tolkien: An Imaginative Life": Lecture series presented at Westminster College, Salt Lake City, UT, March 2009. http://www.gnosis.org/tolkien/lecture1/index.html.

———. "Tolkien, Jung, and the Imagination." Interview with

Miguel Conner. *AeonBytes Gnostic Radio*, April 2011. http://gnosis.org/audio/Tolkien-Interview-with-Owens.mp3.

Scull, Christina and Wayne G. Hammond. *Chronology.* Vol. 1 of *The J. R. R. Tolkien Companion and Guide*. New York: Houghton Mifflin, 2006.

———. *Reader's Guide*. Vol. 2 of *The J. R. R. Tolkien Companion and Guide*. New York: Houghton Mifflin, 2006.

Shippey, Tom. *The Road to Middle-Earth: How J. R. R. Tolkien Created a New Mythology*. New York: Houghton Mifflin, 2003.

Tolkien, J. R. R. *The Adventures of Tom Bombadil*. Edited by Christina Scull and Wayne G. Hammond. London: HarperCollins, 2014.

———. *Beowulf*, edited by Christopher Tolkien. New York: Houghton Mifflin, 2014.

———. *Beren and Lúthien*, edited by Christopher Tolkien. New York: Houghton Mifflin, 2017.

———. *The Children of Húrin*, edited by Christopher Tolkien. New York: Houghton Mifflin, 2008.

———. *The Fall of Gondolin*, edited by Christopher Tolkien. New York: Houghton Mifflin, 2018.

———. *The Histories of Middle-Earth*. Volumes 1-12, edited by Christopher Tolkien. London: HarperCollins, 2002.

———. *The Hobbit: Or There and Back Again*. Boston: Houghton Mifflin, 1991.

———. *The Letters of J. R. R. Tolkien*, edited by Humphrey Carpenter, with Christopher Tolkien. New York: Houghton Mifflin, 2000.

———. *The Lord of the Rings*. New York: Houghton Mifflin, 1994.

———. "The Lost Road." In *The History of Middle-Earth: The Lost Road and Other Writings*. Vol. 5, edited by Christopher Tolkien, 36-104. New York: Houghton Mifflin, 2010.

———. *The Monsters and the Critics*, edited by Christopher Tolkien. London: HarperCollins, 2006.

———. "The Music of Ainur." In *The History of Middle-Earth: The Book of Lost Tales, Part I*. Vol. 1, edited by Christopher Tolkien, 45-63. New York: Houghton Mifflin, 2010.

———. "The Notion Club Papers." In *The History of Middle-Earth: Sauron Defeated*. Vol. 9, edited by Christopher Tolkien, 145–327. New York: Houghton Mifflin, 2010.

———. *On Fairy-Stories*, edited by Verlyn Flieger and Douglas A. Anderson. London: HarperCollins, 2014.

———. *The Silmarillion*, edited by Christopher Tolkien. New York: Houghton Mifflin, 2001.

———. *Sir Gawain and the Green Knight, Pearl, and Sir Orfeo*. London: HarperCollins, 1995.

———. *Smith of Wootton Major*, edited by Verlyn Flieger. London: HarperCollins, 2005.

———. *Tales from the Perilous Realm*. London: HarperCollins, 1997.

———. "The Tale of Eärendel." In *The History of Middle-Earth: The Book of Lost Tales, Part II*. Vol. 2, edited by Christopher Tolkien, 252-77. New York: Houghton Mifflin, 2010.

———. "The Theft of Melko." In *The History of Middle-Earth: The Book of Lost Tales, Part I*. Vol. 1, edited by Christopher Tolkien, 140-61. New York: Houghton Mifflin, 2010.

———. *The Tolkien Reader*. New York: Ballantine, 1966.

———. *Unfinished Tales: Of Númenor and Middle-Earth*, edited by Christopher Tolkien. New York: Houghton Mifflin, 1980.

Unwin, Rayner. "Early Days of Elder Days." In *Tolkien's Legendarium: Essays on The History of Middle-Earth*, edited by Verlyn Flieger and Carl F. Hostetter. Westport, CT: Greenwood Press, 2000.

Wain, John Barrington. *Sprightly Running: Part of an Autobiography*. New York: St. Martin's, 1962.

Zaleski, Philip and Carol Zaleski. *The Fellowship: The Literary Lives of the Inklings*. New York: Farrar, Straus and Giroux, 2015.

About Nura Learning

Nura Learning is an online learning platform founded in 2017 by Jeremy Johnson, and the Nuralogical book series is a co-creative effort between Nura Learning and Revelore Press to bring the content of the courses into physical text form. Nura Learning draws together consciousness studies, integral philosophy, and imaginal studies, and is situated in the lineage of such educational institutions as the California Institute of Integral Studies (where I did my graduate work), Goddard College, the Lindisfarne Association, and Auroville.

In the autumn months of 2018 I offered my first course at Nura, "Journey to the Imaginal Realm: Reading J.R.R. Tolkien's *The Lord of the Rings*" to an enthusiastic group of almost seventy students. Since then I have also taught another course on Tolkien's work, "Sub-Creating Middle-earth: Reading J. R. R. Tolkien's *The Silmarillion*." In conjunction with the publication of this book, I will be presenting the course on *The Lord of the Rings* once more, with the intention of the class becoming an annual offering. This reader's guide is a companion to the course, and if you find yourself enjoying this book I would warmly invite you to join one of Nura Learning's courses, to deepen your engagement with the vast world of the imagination in a devoted community of learning. B.T.

Lightning Source UK Ltd.
Milton Keynes UK
UKHW012248050620
364507UK00004B/873